all

we

have

is

# all

# we

# have

# is

# now

## LISA SCHROEDER

Point

Copyright © 2015 by Lisa Schroeder

All rights reserved. Published by Point, an imprint of Scholastic Inc., *Publishers since 1920*. SCHOLASTIC, POINT, and associated logos are trademarks and/or registered trademarks of Scholastic Inc.

Library of Congress Cataloging-in-Publication Data

Schroeder, Lisa, author.
    All we have is now / Lisa Schroeder.
        pages cm
    ISBN 978-0-545-80253-6
    1. Conduct of life—Juvenile fiction. 2. Friendship—Juvenile fiction.
3. Families—Oregon—Portland—Juvenile fiction. 4. Portland (Or.)—Juvenile
fiction. [1. Conduct of life—Fiction. 2. Friendship—Fiction. 3. Family life—
Oregon—Portland—Fiction. 4. Portland (Or.)—Fiction.] I. Title.
    PZ7.S3818Al 2015
    [Fic]—dc23

                                                          2014038372

10 9 8 7 6 5 4 3 2 1                    15 16 17 18 19 20

Printed in the U.S.A.              23
First printing, August 2015
Book design by Yaffa Jaskoll

for Sara Larson and Candace Robinson,
thanks for all of the support over the years,

and

for Mrs. Smith, my favorite high school teacher,
who asked the question, if you only had 24 hours . . .

NO ONE saw it coming.
Because this particular
cosmic death star
came from the direction
of the sun,
we were blind.

And then, by some miracle,
an astronomer spotted it.
A killer asteroid,
coming right for us
and due to hit Idaho
in a matter of weeks.
The devastation would
affect the United States
as well as parts of Canada
and Mexico.

*Space, the final frontier.*

The place most people
don't think about much because,
after all, it's out there and we are here,
and for millions of years

the earth has occupied its own little part
of the universe with very few
dramatic incidents.
Until now.

For a couple of weeks,
it was pure pandemonium.
Impossible to describe.
Innocent people killed
because of the chaos
in airports and
on the roads
as many tried
to make their escape.

*Get the hell out of Dodge.*

For soon, the land of the free
and the home of the brave
would be the land
that was struck with an explosion
a hundred times greater than the biggest
nuclear bomb ever detonated.

*Fasten your seat belts.*
*It's going to be a bumpy ride.*

Like the *Titanic*, some got away.
Some were safe.
Some would live.
Others would not.

"I DON'T think I can stand the waiting any longer," Emerson tells Vince. "I mean, what's the point? It's basically over."

She sits across from him, on an empty bed, as he throws a small bouncy ball at the wall.

*Bounce. Catch.*

*Bounce. Catch.*

*Bounce. Catch.*

The guy couldn't sit still if his life depended on it. When they panhandled, he had this crazy thing he did with his feet, shuffling back and forth and side to side as he held the sign they'd made that said, WE'RE HOMELESS AND HUNGRY. ANY LITTLE BIT HELPS. THANK YOU AND GOD BLESS. Vince just likes to be moving, somehow, someway.

They've been in this youth shelter for two weeks. It's nice. For the most part, Emerson loves it. She's had a bed with a pillow and a shower every morning. The hardest part has been figuring out what to do with all the extra time. A silly problem that is only temporary, she realizes.

Before, they slept in parks, in alleyways, in backyard sheds. They scrounged for food in restaurant dumpsters, or begged for money on the street. Every day, it was about survival. It was a dirty, ugly life, but they became pros at living that way.

When the news hit and things got crazy, Vince found this place, and fortunately, there was room. A lot of the kids had left, hoping to return to their families or catch rides to the northeastern states. Hard to know if it would be far enough, but most people didn't want to sit around and do nothing.

Emerson jumps up and catches the ball. She sits down next to Vince. Her best friend. Her confidant. Her brother on the streets.

He reaches over and takes the ball from her hand. He has big hands. Big feet, too. The kind you see on professional basketball players. She's often wondered if he ever had any desire to play. But she's never asked. If he'd said yes, all it would have done is made them both feel bad. She tries to avoid that happening as much as possible.

"Yeah, I've been thinking about it," Vince says. "Maybe it's best if we go out on our terms. Decide how and when, you know?"

Emerson looks for fear or sadness in his eyes, but there is none. Not that she can see anyway. If it's true, if he isn't afraid, he's in a much different place than she is. Although, it's not just this day that she feels afraid, it's every day, really. Afraid of getting discovered and sent home, but also afraid of living on the streets forever. Afraid of getting hurt again the way her family hurt her, but also afraid she'll never love anyone ever again. The fear is always there, buzzing around in her head like an annoying fly that keeps bumping up against the window, trying to find a way out. Mostly, she tries her best to ignore it.

"The question is," Vince continues, "whether you want quiet or dramatic."

She raises an eyebrow. "Quiet? Like, what, we find our-selves some Nerf guns?"

He sits up and gives her knee a little shove. "You know what I mean."

"Well, what do you want to do?"

His eyes stay locked onto hers, but she looks away. Not because she's embarrassed or self-conscious. God, not with Vince. He's seen her at her worst, more times than she'd like to admit. They've gone days without washing themselves. Weeks, a few times. What a sight she must have been. Stringy, greasy hair. Zits on her face. Dirt caked underneath her fin-gernails. She studies her hands now, small but strong, and most of all, clean, thankfully. It's a relief to look in the mirror now and not be ashamed of the image she sees, with full, shiny hair and her blue eyes bright and well rested.

No, it's just that sometimes, Vince looks at her like he wants to spill the contents of his heart at her feet. He's like the old jukebox at her dad's place that sits there quietly until someone puts a quarter into it. So she looks away because she doesn't want him to think she has a quarter to give when she doesn't. She's broke. In more ways than one.

As she avoids his gaze, Vince seems to wrestle with the best way to answer her question. Finally, he says, "I just want it to be . . . easy."

Emerson nods. He's nailed it. Because sitting around, waiting, for the next twenty-eight hours does not sound easy. "I was thinking the bridge," she says softly. "You and me. On the count of three."

He tilts his head slightly. Studies her as he considers this idea. "Like little kids, jumping in the pool."

Right. Except there's no water under Suicide Bridge. Only cold, hard pavement. City officials erected a barrier a few years back, to try to prevent people from jumping, but it didn't work as well as they'd hoped. People who are determined just climb around the barrier.

Emerson tries to imagine grabbing Vince's hand, and jumping with him. Happy-go-lucky Vince, in his Charlie Brown shirt. She'd found it last week underneath a bed. Someone left it behind. It's yellow, with a big black squiggle at the belly. It makes Emerson smile when she remembers how thrilled he was when she gave it to him.

"The yellow looks good against your dark skin," she told him.

"Charlie Brown should have been a black kid," he said. "That *Peanuts* gang needs a little diversity."

"There's a black kid," Emerson argued. "But he didn't get much airtime. I can't even remember his name."

"See? So typical. Put him in the background, out of the way, because that's where someone like him, like me, belongs, right?"

Though Emerson isn't black, she'd related to his comment, because she often felt like a background character in her own life. Hell, in her own *home*. Well, what used to be her home, anyway.

It hadn't been so bad when she was younger. When her dad still lived with them, and they were a normal family. In fact, she and her dad both adored Charlie Brown. And Lucy and Schroeder, too. Every year, they'd watched the Charlie Brown Christmas special together.

She quickly pushes the thoughts away. The last thing she needs right now is to take a sentimental trip down memory lane. It won't help anything. In fact, she's pretty sure it will only make things worse.

"Okay," Vince says, interrupting the silence. "Whatever you want is fine with me."

"When?" Emerson asks, nervously picking at a loose thread on her jean shorts. "When should we do it?"

"I don't know."

She looks up and stares at him. Tries not to think about what it's going to be like. Whether there will be any pain before the peace.

"Soon, I think," she says, tucking her straight brown hair behind her ears. "Soon would be better. For me, anyway."

"Okay."

She takes a deep breath. "Okay. So do we just . . . go? Leave our stuff here?"

"Yeah. It's not like we have much anyway, right? Anything you want to do first?"

She looks out the window. Late summer in Portland is the best. If they hurry, they can make it before it gets dark.

Death at sunset sounds nice.

"No," she says. "If you haven't noticed by now, there's nothing here for me." She pauses. "Except you, of course."

EMERSON IS surprised by how empty the streets are. Of course there are other homeless people, wandering around, like always. But very few cars. It's so different from how it was ten days ago, when people took to the streets protesting the government's lack of response. For a few nights, things got pretty violent, and Emerson and Vince hid out in the shelter, waiting for it to pass.

The quiet and stillness is strange, but also a nice change. As she thinks about it, it makes sense, really. The shops, banks, and restaurants seem to be closed now. There's no reason to do business, after all. The people who couldn't leave are probably at home, spending their last hours with loved ones.

It's like a holiday. Like Thanksgiving, but without football or Black Friday ads. Maybe some people are even cooking turkeys and pumpkin pies.

God, pumpkin pie. It's been a long time since Emerson's had pumpkin pie with real whipped cream. She left home the spring she'd turned sixteen. It seems like yesterday and, at the same time, like a hundred lifetimes ago.

But it all ends now.

She won't live to see her eighteenth birthday. For her seventeenth birthday, Vince stole a couple of doughnuts from the supermarket. Took them out of the case, put them in a plastic bag, and stuffed them inside his coat.

"Happy birthday," he said as he handed the bag to her. "Sorry it's not a cake."

"Go back there and stick a cake in your pants," Emerson demanded.

"You want to eat a cake that's been in my pants?"

"Never mind. I'll take the doughnuts." She smiled up at him. Literally, up at him, since he towers above her five-foot-three frame.

They have a ways to walk to reach the Vista Bridge. But it's a nice evening. Not too hot, and there's a soft breeze. Emerson lifts her face and looks at the baby-blue sky, dotted with clouds.

"I wonder how close the asteroid has to be before we can see it," Emerson says.

"I read an article in the final edition of the newspaper that said it's really dark, with not a lot of light bouncing off it, so we shouldn't expect to see it. Not until it's super close, anyway."

"As in, 'Watch out, here it comes'?"

"Pretty much."

They walk past the old historic church, one of the most beautiful buildings in Portland with its teal doors, stained glass windows, and the elegant tall steeple. Just as Emerson wonders if people are inside, praying, she hears an organ, the sound drifting out of an open window.

The music is kind of sad. Haunting. It gives her chills. She thinks about what it must be like to have faith right now—to believe in something more. Something bigger and better after this. It must be comforting, to be absolutely certain there is nothing to fear. She's tried, a couple of times. To believe. To pray. But when nothing gets better, it's hard to keep it up.

"Do you wish now we'd tried to leave?" Emerson asks.

"Nah. The shelter's been nice, right? Better than the Ritz."

When they'd heard the news, they'd stayed up all night, talking about what they wanted to do. The truth was, they were tired. Tired of working so hard just to get up every day and live the same filthy, miserable life over and over again. Tired of running from the ghosts of their pasts, the pimps on the streets, and the security officers in the stores they occasionally stole from.

Tired.

Emerson recalls the day they arrived at the shelter. "God, the first hot shower I took in that place might have been the best thing in my entire life."

"No doubt. You know, maybe heaven will be one long, hot shower. With lots of soap. And hot girls. And—"

"Stop," Emerson says with a laugh. "You need to keep those heavenly fantasies to yourself, all right?"

"Em, you could be one of them." He pauses, like he's trying to decide if he should say it. Or if he should shut up and wait for that quarter Emerson never seems to have. This time, he continues. Maybe he decides life is too short to keep waiting. "The only one, actually. Just say the word."

She can feel his eyes on her. "No way. I shower alone or not at all. I'm selfish when it comes to hot water."

"Well, that's disappointing to hear."

She's learned it's easiest to joke about it with him. In truth, there've been a few times it could have been more. But Emerson wouldn't let it happen. She'd needed Vince to be her friend. More than anything, that's what she'd needed. And she'd told him that, in no uncertain terms. Nothing could happen between them. Ever. Her life was messy enough; she didn't need him making it even messier.

"Maybe in heaven, you'll finally stop running from me," he says softly.

She scoffs. "Believe me, if we make it to heaven, running is the last thing I'll be doing. I want a comfy chair and all of the ice cream I can eat."

"Good. We can share."

"Maybe. But only if you have your own spoon."

AS THEY wind their way up into the Portland Heights area, on a footpath they discovered one day while exploring the neighborhood, Emerson says, "I wonder how long of a drop it is from the bridge to the street below."

"Over a hundred feet," Vince says. "Easily."

They reach the top of the path and turn onto a narrow residential street. The houses here are older, yet elegant. They walk along quietly, and Emerson thinks about the families inside the homes. Have any of them considered what Vince and Emerson have planned? After all, Suicide Bridge is right in their backyard. Although, why would they do that when they have their lovely houses filled with their favorite things, and their favorite people, too? It's different for them. Vince and Emerson have none of that.

"Check this out," Vince says as they reach a yard that is filled with a forest of bamboo that towers above the roofs in the neighborhood. "Man, that is cool. I've never seen anything like it."

"Even up here," Emerson says as they continue walking, "in this amazing neighborhood, we're reminded that Portland is weird."

"Which is why we fit in so well."

"Hey, weirdo, speak for yourself."

At the end of the street, they turn onto Vista Avenue. They've made it. Emerson can't help but think how ugly, how completely out of place the black barricade fencing looks next to the pretty old stone railing of the bridge. It's definitely a lot more work now to jump.

"Let's go to the middle of the street and look out, over the city," Vince says. "It's an awesome view, and with the sun setting soon . . ."

His voice trails off when they suddenly realize they aren't the only ones at the bridge. A tall, good-looking man is on the other side of the barricade holding on to the fence and inching his way along the shorter stone railing, when he sees them. Emerson grabs on to Vince's arm.

Vince's voice is calm and reassuring. He is a rock, like always. "It's all right. He can go first. We're in no hurry, right?"

An image pops into Emerson's brain, and it's so horrible, she stops. Squeezes Vince's arm even tighter. "But . . . his body will be down there. Vince, I don't know if I can—"

And then, the man changes direction until he reaches the end where he can climb down onto the street. As he walks toward them, Emerson's heart races. What does he want? Why didn't he go through with it? Does he want them to leave?

He raises his hand, like a friendly wave. "Hello."

"Hey," Vince says. "We're sorry. We didn't mean to, uh, bother you."

"No, it's okay. I'm glad you're here, actually."

This makes Emerson even more nervous. He wants something from them. But the question is, what?

When the man reaches them, he extends his hand to Vince. "I'm Carl."

He's middle-aged. Probably close in age to Emerson's father. His brown hair is thick and his eyes are kind. He reminds Emerson of Hugh Jackman. For some reason, this thought alone relaxes her a little.

"I'm Vince, and this is Emerson."

"It's good to meet you," Carl says with a smile. "Really good. This means I can maybe do one more. That is, if you'll let me. I'd love to help you."

Emerson shakes her head. "One more what?"

"Sorry," Carl says. "Let me explain. Yesterday, a man I'd never met before asked me what I might wish for. Something I hadn't done in life that I'd always wanted to do. I told him since I was a little boy, I'd always dreamed of being a fireman. I couldn't pursue it because my father insisted I join him in his landscaping business. But yesterday, we went into the fire station, got dressed in the gear, and took the fire truck out for a spin." He stops and closes his eyes for a moment, like the memory is a sweet piece of candy that's almost gone. When he opens his eyes, he continues, "I swore I'd do the same for five more people. I managed four and thought I might find my last one here. But no one came. And then, I just felt ready, you know? Ready to say good-bye. At peace, I suppose. But then, here you are."

Emerson doesn't know what to say. Vince says, "I'm not sure I'm following you."

"Is there something you want?" Carl asks, his voice warm and soothing. "Anything I can do for you? That's all. It's simple, really."

Before Emerson can speak, Vince says, "Every day since I've been on the streets, all I've wanted is cash. You know, money for food. Shelter. Clothes. A car to take us places.

We've had nothing for a long time, and it's hard, man. It's so incredibly hard, I can't even tell you."

It's true. And yet at the same time, Emerson can't believe what she's hearing. What can money possibly get them now? It's the last thing they should be asking for. But before she can argue, before she can say, "Wait, let's think about this," the man reaches into his back pocket and pulls out a wallet. He hands it over to Vince.

"Take this," he says. "Feel rich in these final hours."

Vince opens the wallet as Emerson peers over his arm. It's packed full of bills. He pulls one out, and Benjamin Franklin stares up at them. A hundred bucks. And that's just one.

"I don't know," Vince says, shoving the bill back inside and snapping it closed. "This doesn't seem right. I mean, are you sure you don't want it?"

Carl laughs. He laughs and laughs. "I'm sure. It's yours. Go. Enjoy."

He turns and walks away from them, heading back to the end of the bridge, where he'll climb around the barricade and onto the stone railing.

Emerson looks at Vince. "Should we stop him?"

Before Vince can respond, Carl shouts to them, "Pay it forward, if you can. Look for those who have wishes or regrets."

Panic rises up, and Emerson realizes she doesn't want to be here. She starts to run, heading back the way they came. Vince yells something, but she's covered her ears with her hands. She doesn't want to hear the fall. Definitely doesn't want to see it.

She remembers Vince's words. *I just want it to be easy.*

There is nothing easy about this, she realizes. Not a single thing.

*THE SUN* sets
and the sky turns
a pale shade of tangerine

just for a moment.

A golden hue
falls across the city,
and if time could stop,

now would be the perfect time.

The majestic scene is
both inspiring and comforting,
and everything feels right

even when it's not.

People around the city
stop and take in
this glorious golden moment

and wish for days they miss already.

Then, it's gone.
There is only grayness
that eventually turns to black,

because it's true what they say.

Nothing lasts forever.

CARL STANDS there for a while, watching the sky change colors as the sun slips away. A flood of emotions washes over him, thinking about what comes next.

Fear.

Sadness.

Loneliness.

Regret.

But also happiness, because it's been a good life. He thought he was ready, but as darkness descends, he's not so sure. Maybe he could help more people. Maybe a miracle will happen. Maybe . . .

His phone buzzes in his pocket. Gripping the barricade with one hand, he pulls it out of his pocket and says, "Hello?"

"Carl? It's me. Where are you?"

He won't tell her. It'd upset her and she'd blame herself. He decides to keep it simple. "Downtown. Where are you?"

She can barely get the word out. "Home."

This isn't what he expected her to say. "Which home?"

"Ours," she says. "I spent time with my parents, hugged them good-bye, and came back here. I drove all night and all day. They didn't want me to go, of course, but I decided here was where I wanted to be most. With you."

"Oh my God," Carl says, suddenly clutching the railing harder. "Trinity. I—"

"You'll come home now, right?"

His brain is on overdrive, trying to process this latest development. "I gave away my car. And my wallet."

"What do you mean, gave them away?" she asks. "Why?"

"I, um, I wanted to do something. To help people. I don't know. Anyway, can you come get me?"

She starts to cry. "No, I can't. The car ran out of gas, because it's practically impossible to find fuel. I had to walk the last few miles. I didn't call you because I wanted to surprise you, but then you weren't here."

"Shhh, it's okay, Trinity. We'll figure something out. Can you check with the neighbors? See if any of them are home? And if they aren't, see if you can get into a garage. Surely cars have been left behind. I'll see what I can do on my end, too. Maybe I can catch a ride with someone."

"Carl, you have to get here."

"I know, honey. I know. Call me if you find a car you can drive, all right?"

"Okay. 'Bye."

" 'Bye."

He stuffs the phone in his pocket and inches back the way he came, until he's on solid ground again. As he stops to collect himself, he notices someone has written something in chalk on the sidewalk. Funny how he didn't notice it before.

*Tomorrow is a new day. I want you to be here for it. Please let someone help you.*

EMERSON RUSHES down the narrow street, past the lovely houses and the bamboo-filled yard. It's not pitch-black out yet, thank goodness, so she can see where she's going.

"Em, wait up," Vince calls, but she waves him off and keeps up her brisk pace. She doesn't feel like talking. Because what is there to say? People are dying, afraid of what happens next. And more people will die tomorrow. A lot more. The unfairness of it all suddenly makes her want to scream with rage.

Why didn't the government do more to help everyone? Why wasn't there an evacuation plan put in place? Why did it have to be every man for himself? Sure, there wasn't much time, but there was *some* time. A little bit. Wasn't it enough? Why couldn't it have been enough? It all just seems wildly insane and it makes her feel insane that she is here, living in this nightmare.

When she finally gets back down to Jefferson Street, she stops to catch her breath. Vince reaches for her and gently touches her arm. "Hey. Are you okay?"

"Not really, no."

"Yeah. I get it. All of a sudden it feels a lot more real or something."

Emerson shudders. Vince tries to put his arm around her,

to pull her close, like this will help, but she spins away, dodging the gesture.

After all, it's every man for himself. That's the way it has to be. Anything different will make things too complicated. More frightening. Because any time, he could change his mind. *Any time.*

And then what?

Vince speaks softly, like he's talking to a frightened kitten. "Come on. There's that little tavern down the street here. Let's see if the doors might be open. We can sit down. Maybe find something to eat."

She follows him down the sidewalk, along the eerily quiet street until they come to the Goose Hollow Inn. It's a funky little place, with a wooden porch along the front and an even bigger outside eating area along the side. He motions for her to take a seat at the table near the door while he tries the knob, but it's locked. He sits across from her.

"I'm worried about you," he says. "Can you tell me what's going on inside that head of yours?"

He asks her this sometimes. But just like always, she'll only give him a fraction of the answer. She leans forward, rubbing her face with her hands. "What were we thinking? We can't do that. I mean, how could he possibly do that?"

Vince doesn't say anything. He probably knows she doesn't really expect an answer. She decides she doesn't want to talk about it anymore. They made a mistake. It's over. Time to move on.

She eyes the wallet in his hands. "Vince, I don't understand. Why'd you ask for money?" There's a streetlight nearby, so she can see his face, and she stares at the person she's come to know so well, and yet, she never saw that coming.

He shakes his head as he puts the wallet on the table. "I don't know. I was just being honest, that's all. Didn't really think it through. You're not mad, are you?"

Emerson turns and stares at the empty street. She's always admired Vince's honesty. Can't get upset at him for that. She looks at him again and gives him a little smile. "No. Just wondering what we're going to do with a wallet full of money. Take a trip to New York City, maybe? Have some pizza and see a show?"

"You have to admit, that'd be fun." He opens the wallet and takes out all the bills. "It feels nice to have it, even if there isn't much we can do with it now. Here." He hands it to her. "See for yourself."

She runs her hands across the bills. Fans them out. Starts to count them, but stops herself. It doesn't matter. It's something they haven't had for so long, but she'd rather have something else. Something a little more meaningful.

"I'm sorry I spoke up first," Vince says, as if he can hear her thoughts. "I should have let you say something."

Emerson hands the money back to him, and he slips it in the wallet. "It's fine. It's what came to mind, and any other time, it would have made a lot of sense. But right now . . ."

She doesn't have to say it. He knows. It's basically worthless.

Vince slides the driver's license out of the wallet and starts reading.

"Carl Ragsdale. Fifty-one years old. Six feet, two inches. Two hundred and ten pounds. Lives in Lake Oswego."

"I wonder why he wasn't with his family," Emerson ponders out loud.

Vince puts the driver's license back where it belongs. "Yeah, that is odd. After all, Lake Oswego is the capital of suburbia. He must have a family. Unless they all left, and he stayed behind for some reason?"

Emerson shrugs. "We'll probably never know." She leans back in her chair and takes a deep breath. There's a slight hint of cigarette smoke in the air. "So what do we do now?"

"I've been thinking about that, and you know, I like what he was doing, Em."

"What do you mean?"

"Helping people. Making dreams come true or whatever. I mean, think about it for a second. We've been living in survival mode for a long time. Maybe it's time to have some fun while we help people do the same. If anyone deserves it, we do."

Emerson considers his words. She doesn't feel like she deserves anything. She's felt worthless for so long, it's hard to feel like that's changed.

When she doesn't answer, Vince leans across the table, his arms stretched out. She can tell he wants her to take his hands, even after she'd pushed him away earlier. It wasn't very nice, the way she acted. He'd only been trying to comfort her. To help her. That's what friends do, after all. So this time, she doesn't refuse. His hands are rough. Strong. Soothing.

"Come on. Let's try it," he says, rubbing his thumbs across the top of her hands. It gives her goose bumps, and she quickly pulls her hands away.

"Try it, how?" she asks, pretending to scratch an itch on her arm.

"We'll help one person, and see what happens. If it's weird or it makes you feel uncomfortable, then we're through. It's over and that's that."

Before she can respond, a kid comes from around the corner, smoking a cigarette. She can't tell how old he might be. He's got a baseball hat on and a Lakers basketball jersey that's too big for him. He stops. Stares. Then he asks, "Do you know if I can get into this place? I was hoping I might get something to drink."

Vince stands up. "The front door is locked up tight."

The kid shakes his head as he throws the cigarette on the ground and crushes it with his shoe.

"You all right?" Vince asks.

He doesn't look at them as he replies. "I—I couldn't stay there. With them. I just . . . I couldn't, you know? I snuck out the bathroom window."

"Your family's at home?" Emerson asks.

He nods as he blinks a bunch of times. Like he's trying to keep it together.

Emerson glances at Vince. She knows what he's thinking. This kid's the one.

"It's okay, man," Vince says. "Sometimes we have to do what's right for ourselves, even if others don't agree."

"Yeah," the kid says. "I felt smothered there. Like I couldn't breathe or something."

"I know," Emerson says. She waves her hand at Vince. "We both understand."

"You can hang with us for a while, if you want to," Vince says. "Though I guess we should introduce ourselves. I'm Vince and this is Emerson. We've been living on the streets for the past year and a half."

The kid looks at them differently. "Seriously?"

"Yep," Emerson says as she stands up. "Seriously. What's your name?"

"Hayden."

"Let me ask you something, Hayden," Vince says. "What'd you dream about doing? Someday? You know, when you got out of school."

"What's it matter now?"

"It matters to us," Emerson says.

"You'll think it's stupid."

"No," Emerson responds. "We won't. Right now, there isn't anything that's stupid."

"Yep," Vince agrees. "She speaks the truth."

Hayden seems to consider this for a few seconds before he says, "I play the guitar. And I sing, too. I've always thought it'd be cool to be in a band."

Emerson smiles. She likes this answer, though she's not sure how they can possibly pull a band together for him now. "So basically, you want to be a rock-and-roll star? Play music, travel the world, and get the chicks?"

Hayden chuckles. "Um, okay. Sure. That sounds good."

Vince grabs the wallet off the table and puts it in his pocket. "Let's see if we can find a way into this place. Get some food. Then we'll see what we can do for you. Make a plan, you know? I have an idea or two."

"What do you mean?" Hayden asks.

"Never mind. We'll explain later. For now, you hungry?"

"Yeah. I'm starving. They were pulling a turkey out of the oven when I left."

"I knew it," Emerson mutters under her breath.

"What's that?" Hayden asks.

"Nothing," Emerson says quickly. "So, what's the deal, you're not a fan of turkey?"

"Can't stand it," Hayden says. "My grandma always

overcooks it. Like she's afraid of poisoning us if she doesn't cook it long enough."

"Ah yes, turkey that tastes like a shoe," Emerson says. "So appetizing, isn't it? Were they going to have pie, too?"

"Nah. Just some cookies my mom made."

"What kind?"

"Oatmeal with raisins. I think they're trying to use up whatever's in the cupboard."

Emerson starts to say how ridiculous that sounds, but she realizes practical people probably can't suddenly become impractical. With all of the talk of food, she decides she's hungry, too.

They go around to the side door. It's open.

THE PLACE isn't very big. It is, however, dark and extremely stuffy. Vince props the door open to let in some fresh air.

"We need to find a light switch," Emerson says, feeling her way around the small kitchen area behind the bar.

"How come more people aren't looting places like they were last week?" Hayden asks.

"My guess is because what most people want right now is to be with their families," Vince replies. "Oh, here's the switch."

Once they have light, Vince opens the refrigerator and starts pulling tubs out and putting them on the counter.

"How long you think this stuff has been in there?" Emerson asks. Then she sees dates written in black marker on tape. "Oh, they're all from the end of August, so just a couple of weeks ago."

"Just?" Hayden asks. "Is food poisoning part of your plan, then?"

Emerson laughs. "You know what? I like you, Hayden. And please don't worry. We've eaten much worse and lived to tell about it. It'll be fine. We'll make sure we choose wisely."

All three of them start popping the lids off the containers. "I think this is vegetable soup," Vince says.

"Soup. Great," Emerson says. "Just what we need when it's about a hundred and twenty degrees in here."

"This salad looks gross," Hayden says, slapping the lid back on and pushing it away.

Emerson studies the contents of another container. "Now, this looks promising."

"What is it?" Vince asks, peering over her shoulder.

"Pretty sure it's pulled pork. See if you can find any rolls or bread in the freezer, would you? We can defrost them in the microwave. And I'll start heating this up."

Twenty minutes later, the three of them are sitting at a table lit with candles, sipping on ice-cold sodas and eating pulled pork sandwiches.

"The candles are a nice touch," Vince says as he wipes his mouth.

"You know me," Emerson says. "Classy with a capital C."

"I have to say, this is a lot better than turkey," Hayden mumbles, his mouth full.

Vince nods. "Yeah, best sandwich I've had in years. Nice job, Em."

Hayden downs the rest of his drink. "So, if you don't mind me asking, how come you guys aren't with your families? I know you said you've been living on the streets, but don't you want to see them now? Before . . . you know."

Emerson waits, curious as to how much Vince will reveal. He hates talking about his life. Whatever's happened to him, he's made it very clear from day one that Emerson shouldn't ask about anything. He told her, if he feels like sharing, he will. Otherwise, it needs to stay right where it belongs—in the past.

She's actually a bit surprised when he answers Hayden matter-of-factly. "I don't have a family. Never knew my dad, and my mom died when I was eight. I was in foster care for years before I got fed up and ran."

"That sucks," Hayden says. "I mean, I'm sorry. About your mom."

"Yeah. Thanks."

"What about you?" Hayden looks at Emerson.

She considers telling him the story. About how her parents split up when she was twelve. How she and her older sister lived with their mom for a couple of years, visiting their dad every other weekend, until her mom got a new boyfriend and got pregnant. How he and Emerson didn't get along at all, until finally, her mom said she had to go live with her dad. How it tore her up that her mother would choose a man over her own daughter. How her dad was super strict, and how she got angrier and angrier, seeing how much her mom loved her new baby daughter, but didn't seem to give a shit about Emerson. How her dad talked about sending her to some camp in Colorado for troubled teens. How she just wanted to get away from all of them.

Well, almost all of them.

But she doesn't say any of that. "It's complicated. The only person I really miss is my older sister, Frankie. I'd love to see her again, but I'm not sure she'd keep it a secret if I got in touch with her."

"Maybe you should try," Hayden says. "I might be able to help if you—"

Emerson interrupts him. "Nah. Don't worry about it. It's okay."

"So how come your family didn't leave, Hayden?" Vince asks before he takes another bite of his sandwich.

"No passports," Hayden explains. "I guess countries that

won't be affected by the asteroid had to draw the line somewhere. It'd be impossible to take everybody, right?"

"Seems like they could have at least tried," Emerson says, picking up one of the candles and pouring some of the hot wax onto the tablecloth.

"Who knows how far the blast will go?" Vince says. "What it will do to the oceans, the atmosphere, everything. My guess? No one is safe. People are just hoping they are, but I bet it will be a nightmare for everyone, everywhere."

Emerson groans. "Okay, Mr. Tell-It-Like-It-Is, could we perhaps find a subject that is a little less depressing to talk about?" She tilts her head in Hayden's direction. "Impressionable minds and all that."

"You say that like I'm twelve," Hayden says.

"How old are you, anyway?" Emerson asks.

"Sixteen."

"Seriously?" Emerson says. "Wow, you don't look it. Are you sure?"

Hayden chuckles. "I can prove it. My beat-up Civic is out on the street." He leans forward a little. "That's what I was trying to tell you. If you want to go see your sister, I can take you."

Emerson shakes her head. Hard. "No. That's not the plan. The plan is that we help you somehow." She turns to Vince, hoping to get things back on track. "So what exactly *is* the plan?"

## CANNON BEACH
was their special
place.

The girls loved it there.

Caramel corn and taffy.
Haystack Rock and tide pools.
Ocean waves and cold toes.

They found two starfish
clinging to the side of a rock,
one purple, one orange,
arms barely touching.

As Emerson snapped a picture,
Frankie said, "That's us.
I'm the purple one.
You're the orange one."

Emerson replied in typical
little-sister fashion.
"But I want to be the purple one."

Later, their dad took a picture
of the two girls, smiling and
arms around each other,
with their hair blown back
from the wind.

Each of the girls got
a copy.

Emerson kept hers,
safely tucking it
between the pages of
the one book she took with her
when she ran.

*Charlie and the Chocolate Factory.*
Frankie's favorite.

CARL MIGHT not have much, but at least he still had his phone. The first thing he did after he talked to Trinity was to call a few friends to see if any of them were home and could come and get him. Two didn't answer and one of them said he was in Seattle with his family.

Just as he was about to try a couple more, he couldn't get a signal. He turned his phone off and on, and tried again, but nothing.

The service had gone out. So much for having something.

Now he makes his way toward downtown, hoping he can find someone to give him a ride. His mind drifts to the young woman, Lonnie, who got his car, and her four-year-old son, Michael. When Carl asked her if there was anything she wanted or needed, Lonnie told him she wanted to take her son to the beach so he could experience the sand and the ocean for the first time. She'd been living in a small apartment and relying on public transportation to get to work for the past five years. The boy's father had been a one-night stand, and Lonnie had never tried to find him to tell him about the baby.

"We've been happy," she told Carl. "Michael is the best kid. I just wish he could have done more. Experienced more, you know?"

33

Carl looked down at the small boy, who was carrying a tattered blanket and a Superman action figure. He imagined the boy's face when he saw the vast ocean for the first time. When he touched the cold water with his little toes. When he learned the beach was the biggest sandbox ever.

"There should be enough gas to get you to Cannon Beach," Carl said as he handed over his car keys. "You know how to drive, right?"

She looked shocked. "Yes, but are you sure about this? I mean, what if you need to get somewhere? What if you decide you want to see something one last time?"

He shook his head. "Nah. I'm good. I want this for you guys." He kneeled down and looked into Michael's big brown eyes. "Go to the beach. Have fun, okay? Build a sand castle for me."

Michael had held up his action figure and said, "Superman."

"Yep, that's him," Carl said. "You hang on tight to him, okay? We might need him to save the world."

"HOLD ON to your microphone," Emerson says as she opens the door to the karaoke bar and hears noises. "I think there are people in here."

She walks in with Vince and Hayden close behind. An older man with gray hair, wearing a dinner jacket and a red-and-yellow polka-dot bow tie, stands at the counter in the lobby.

"Hello," he says. "How may I help you?"

Vince puts his arm around Hayden's shoulders and they step forward. "I don't know how this place works, but this young man has rock-and-roll dreams, and we're trying to help him."

The man nods. "While we do have rooms for private parties, I'm putting everyone into the suite tonight. It holds up to thirty-five people. I think you'll agree that right now, the more the merrier, yes?"

Vince starts to give his approval while Hayden says, "I don't know about that."

"Oh, come on," Emerson says. "This is it. Your one shot. An audience of two is about as exciting as an empty champagne glass."

"Yeah," Vince says. "I say we go with the suite. Maybe you'll find some groupies that way. I mean, come on, rock and roll ain't nothing without groupies, right?"

Vince steps up to the counter. "How much?"

"For tonight, just ten dollars apiece," the man replies.

"Can I ask why you're doing this?" Emerson says as Vince pulls out Carl's wallet for the cash. "Keeping the place open?"

"Well, I guess my answer is, Why not?" the man tells her. "In some ways, it's just another Wednesday night. And like every other night, some people need a place to go to try and leave their worries behind. One thing I've learned over the years is music has incredible healing powers. Think about it. What else is there that can lift your spirits within the span of three minutes? I figured, tonight people could use a little of that. Right?"

Hayden nods slowly. "Wow. That's totally true."

"Besides," the man continues, "there's no doubt in my mind they're going to find a way to keep it from happening. In the meantime, I refuse to panic."

"Business as usual, then," Vince says as he takes his change.

"Yep." The man points them to the suite. "Okay, you're all set. Cell phone service seems to be down, so you'll have to use the remote to choose your songs. There are books in the room with all of the available songs. Find the one you're interested in, punch the corresponding number into the remote, and you're good to go. If you have questions, I'm sure someone in the room will be happy to show you how it works."

"Thanks," the three say simultaneously. They walk toward the closed door.

"What if they don't want us to join them?" Hayden asks. "I mean, they don't know us. They might think we're ruining it for them."

"No, no, no," Vince says. "You got it all wrong, man. You're not ruining it for them. You need to think like the rock-and-roll star that you are. This is going to be a night they will never, ever forget."

THERE ARE about twenty people in the room. Some are sitting, some are standing. At the front and back of the room, there are big flat-screens hung on the wall.

A man and a woman who look to be in their twenties, dressed casually in their shorts and T-shirts, both have a mic and are singing "Love Shack" by the B-52's. Emerson is pretty impressed with how they sound and gives a look of approval to Vince.

It feels like a party in a way, and Emerson is thrown back to a time before the streets, when she'd sneak out at night to find some fun. She craved it back then—the elation, the frenzy, the constant motion of doing something that made it impossible to think too hard about anything. Right now, she can't deny that she's missed having a good time. Life had become so bleak and tedious, just trying to stay alive.

But this room, this group of people, is jubilant, despite everything going on in the world outside these doors. They don't seem to notice the newcomers, or if they do, they don't care. When the chorus starts up, everyone jumps up and joins in, including Emerson, Vince, and Hayden. It's impossible not to. The room hums with emotions as they sing and dance and make the moment all it can be. Emerson feels alive in a way she hasn't in a long time. It feels amazing, and as she looks around, gratitude fills her.

When the song is over, the woman who was singing says, "We have some new people joining us. Can you introduce yourselves?"

Vince speaks for the three of them, and tells the group their names.

"We're glad you're here," the guy says. "And I sincerely mean that."

Three teen girls pop up and the mics are handed over. This time it's "Teenage Dream" by Katy Perry. Again, during the chorus, it's a sing-along and it's loud and crazy and slightly hilarious.

Emerson makes a heart shape with her hands and looks over at Vince as she sings. Then she blows him a kiss.

*You tease*, he mouths. Then he sticks his hand out and makes a come-over-here motion with his finger. She grabs his finger and pushes it back to his side, laughing. He laughs, too, and she can see that he's as happy as she is, in this place that feels like a dream, where all of the fear and worry has been forgotten. Teenage dream, indeed. She feels her heart give a teeny-tiny bit, in the tender place she's closed off for so long. But she turns her attention back to the music, because she doesn't want to think about any of that. She just wants to have fun with her friends.

As the song's winding down, Emerson leans in and says to Hayden, "You should go next."

"I don't know if I can," he replies. "Just thinking about it makes me feel sick. I've never sung in front of anyone but my mom."

Emerson looks at Vince and points at the front of the room, trying to tell him she plans on jumping up there as soon as the song is over. Which she does. She takes the mic as Vince kind of pulls Hayden over to the machine to choose a song.

"Hi," Emerson says. "Um, we came here tonight for our friend Hayden, who loves music, and has big dreams. Some of you can probably relate. Anyway, while he picks a song, can you guys give him some encouragement?"

The room erupts into applause, whistles, and cheers. It doesn't take Hayden long to choose what he wants to sing, and then he reaches out and takes the microphone with shaky hands. The crowd immediately grows quiet. Emerson and Vince return to the audience.

"This is one of my mom's favorite songs," Hayden says. "I've been singing it since I was three."

And then, it starts. Slowly. Quietly. There are cheers of approval before most everyone sits down to listen to the lyrics of the classic song by Queen, "Bohemian Rhapsody."

It's not what Emerson expected. She thought he'd choose something loud and fast right out of the gate. Although she knows the song, and understands it will grow and change and become so much more.

What's really surprising, though, is this kid's voice. It is on pitch and perfect, and the more he sings, the more Emerson feels like she's the one who's been given a gift.

As he sings about not wanting to die, a lump forms in Emerson's throat and she looks over at Vince. She can tell he's trying not to tear up, too. Because Hayden isn't just singing a song, he's singing an anthem about life and death and what it feels like to face the frightening unknown. The song has an almost fantasy feel about it, but Emerson knows the feelings it's brought up are one hundred percent real.

The heartbreaking moment passes and the song speeds up. Everyone is on their feet, singing along again.

The room is electric as they share the lyrics and the rhythm and the emotions of the song with one another. Just like that, Emerson returns to unbridled joy and it feels as if her whole body is expanding from taking it all in. She can't remember the last time she had this much fun.

And then, without even trying, she does.

**THEY USED** to have concerts
in the living room.

       two sisters

After school,
while their mom worked,
Frankie would play the
old Carpenters album
on the turntable and
sing about yesterdays,
rainy days, and Mondays.

       sweet and sad

Usually Emerson sat
and listened to Frankie,
but once in a while,
Frankie would invite her
to join in.

       happy together

They used curling irons
for microphones
and sang it like they meant it.
Emerson told Frankie,
"You're amazing.
You could be a star."

        dreaming big

Frankie smiled and said,
"But there's a million stars.
Maybe I want to be the
one and only moon instead."

THE MOON is bright and beautiful. As Carl walks, he considers his options. He's asked three people for rides, but none of them were heading in that direction and they didn't want to make a special trip. It's ten miles from downtown Portland to Lake Oswego. A long way to walk, but certainly not impossible.

He's been wandering around, trying to find something to drink. All he can think about is how thirsty he is. His throat and lips are so dry, it hurts. His stomach rumbles. The last twenty-four hours, he didn't worry about food or water. It was all about helping as many people as he could and having fun. It didn't matter what happened to him.

But now, things have changed. It matters.

He heads for a drinking fountain up ahead. When he pushes the button, nothing happens. He curses under his breath. There's only one thing left to do. Break into a place for some food and water, unless he can find somewhere with a door open.

*I'll eat and drink*, he tells himself as he takes a right down a street he hasn't been yet. *Rest a little while. After that, I'll walk home.*

With a plan in place, his pace quickens. Up ahead, there's an old man peering into the window of a shop. As Carl gets closer, he sees it's a bakery. There are still baked goods in the window.

Carl stops and stands next to the man. He's much shorter than Carl. Thin and frail, with white hair and glasses. They stand there for a good minute without saying a word. Finally, the old man says, "My wife worked at this bakery for thirty-five years. She passed away last year. I haven't been back since."

Carl doesn't know what to say except, "I'm sorry." Then he turns and holds out his hand. Introduces himself.

"Nice to meet you, Carl. I'm Jerry."

"Would you like to go inside with me?" Carl asks. "Get something to eat?"

Jerry turns back to the window. Carl knows what the older man is thinking. He wishes his wife were inside, ready to greet him with a smile and a Danish.

They stand there in silence for a long time until Jerry finally says, "Do you think we could get the coffeepot working?"

"There are a whole lot of things I can't do right now," Carl replies, "but I'm pretty sure I can do that."

EMERSON, VINCE, and Hayden sing and dance until their throats are raw and their bodies ache. Mr. Bow-tie brings pitchers of water again and again, but it's never enough.

They can't get enough.

Of water.

Of music.

Of life.

When Emerson suggests stepping outside for some fresh air, Vince and Hayden happily agree.

They lean against the wall of the building. The street is dark, but in the sky, the golden crescent moon glows. Emerson takes it all in, her breaths getting slower and deeper. She feels tingly all over. It's like that moment when you step into the cold Pacific Ocean and feel the water splash across your feet, as the silver-tipped waves toss offshore.

It's *such* a good feeling.

Hayden is the first to speak. "Thanks, you guys. That was a blast."

"Wait until you see what we have planned for tomorrow night," Emerson says. "Talk about a blast."

Vince rolls his eyes. "Just ignore her. We're glad you had fun. And man, let me tell you something. You can sing." He holds his fist out. "Seriously."

Hayden bumps Vince's fist with his. "Nah. I'm nothing special. But I think that was just what I needed, you know? Like, exactly what I needed."

"Me too," Emerson says.

"You want to go back in?" Vince asks.

Emerson studies Hayden while he stares at that beautiful moon like it has all the answers to life's questions.

"I think I might head home," Hayden says. He turns and looks at them. "It's nothing personal. I just—"

"It's okay," Emerson says. "You don't have to explain."

Hayden pulls a pack of cigarettes and a lighter out of his pocket. "They've been good parents. Sometimes better than I've deserved."

Vince wipes his forehead with the sleeve of his T-shirt. "No. Don't say that. I bet you've been a good kid."

"I crawled out the freaking bathroom window. What kind of kid does that?"

"The kind who's got a lot on his mind," Emerson says.

"I bet they'll understand." Vince smiles. "They'll probably cuss your ass out when you get home, but they will understand. Tell them what you did. How much fun you had, you know?"

Hayden puffs on the cigarette as he stuffs the pack back in his pocket. "I'm glad I met you guys."

"Same here." Emerson pulls him into a hug. "And just so you know, you have your first official groupies right here."

"Awesome," Hayden says with a smile as Vince comes over and gives him a quick hug, too. "Hey, you guys need a ride anywhere?"

Vince looks at Emerson and she shrugs. "Thanks, but we're good," Vince says.

Hayden starts humming "We Are the Champions" as he waves and turns to leave.

Vince and Emerson hum, too. And they keep humming, even when they can't hear Hayden anymore.

"You sure we shouldn't have gone with him?" Emerson asks as she leans up against the wall again, running her hand through her hair and shaking it out.

"I'm thinking he probably wants to be alone. Clear his head a little bit before he gets home."

Emerson looks curiously at Vince. "What about you?"

"What about me?"

"You need some head-clearing time?"

He shakes his head. "Girl, what are you talking about?" He reaches for her hand. She takes it, and he pulls her away from the wall. "We have more work to do, you and me."

"We do?"

"Yeah. It was good, right? What we did. I think we should do it again."

They start walking. "You're right, Vince. It *was* good."

WHEN THEY get to Burnside, they head east, toward Waterfront Park. As they pass Powell's Books, with its big red-and-white marquee that still has author-signing dates up from early August, Emerson says, "I wish they were open tomorrow. Then we could go in there and buy some books with Carl's money."

They walk under a streetlight, allowing Emerson to see the funny look Vince gives her. "You want to buy books? Now?"

She shrugs. "Sure. Why not? You know, I always dreamed that someday I'd have a house big enough for my own library. Wouldn't that be cool? Like, people would come over and I'd say, 'Let's have a drink in the library,' and they'd be all, 'Wow, you have a library?'"

"So it's not that you like books, you just want to impress people."

"No. I like books. In fact, I *love* books. That's one love Frankie and I shared. Do you know how many times a book saved me from going crazy in my own house?"

"How many?"

She waves her hand. "Honestly? Too many to count."

"So if you could buy a book tomorrow, only one, what kind would you get?"

She doesn't miss a beat. "A funny one. We could take

turns reading it, and make each other laugh. We'd laugh so hard, we'd forget all about the fact that we're going to die in a matter of hours."

"Em, I hate to tell you this, but I don't think there's anyone in the world who is *that* hilarious."

She gives a little grunt of indignation. "Okay, how about a super-suspenseful one? You know, the kind where you can't turn the pages fast enough because you *have* to find out what happens." She pauses a moment. "Like *The Hunger Games*. I read that book in a single day."

"Hm. Yeah, I guess worrying about someone else is a way to stop worrying about yourself. Which is exactly why we need to find more people to help."

They walk past a Vietnamese restaurant with a large GRAND OPENING banner hung above the door. Emerson thinks of the people who worked hard to open their very own restaurant, only to have to close it down because of an impending asteroid. Not from lack of sales. Or food poisoning. Or a pesky ant infestation.

A freaking asteroid.

"Em, it's pretty late. Are you tired?"

Typical Vince. Always making sure she's okay.

"Like I could actually sleep at a time like this? No. I'm all right. Thanks for asking."

They walk for a while in silence, and Emerson's mind starts to drift. She doesn't want to let herself get sad. She can't. It won't do any good now.

So she asks him the questions she's asked him again and again since she's known him. When she needs to feel better about being here, away from them.

"What's my mom doing right now?"

He doesn't take long to answer. He never does. Vince is good at this game. He always knows what to say. "It's after midnight, and normally she'd be sleeping, but tonight, she's up, listening to a little jazz with a glass of wine. She's got the photo albums out, and she's looking at pictures of you and Frankie, when you were little. You know the ones. Opening Christmas presents in your pj's. Baking cookies together. Building a snowman in the front yard." He looks over at her. "That one year when we got a lot of snow. Remember?"

She nods. She remembers. And he's right, they did build a snowman.

"She doesn't hate me?"

"No. No way. She's feeling grateful for the time she had with you."

It makes Emerson feel better. Just like always. When things get quiet, her imagination creates depressing scenarios as she thinks of her family, going about their lives, absolutely thrilled that Emerson isn't there anymore to cause problems for them. Vince's stories help Emerson see other possibilities, ones she wouldn't come up with on her own. Even if, deep down, she doesn't believe the words, she likes hearing them. For a brief moment, she can see a happy movie inside of her head instead of a sad one.

"What's my sister doing?"

"Well, she's with her boyfriend. The one who loves her a lot and is taking good care of her. They're chowing down on a big ole pizza."

Emerson smiles. "Mmmmm. What kind?"

"Canadian bacon and pineapple. Your favorite. She's thinking about you. Hoping you're doing well." He pauses.

"You know, Em, you could try calling your mom's place. Talk to your sister, at least."

"I know." She can't deny it's crossed her mind a few times the past couple of days.

There'd been so many times she'd wanted to call, but there was one thing that always held her back. What if her mom hung up on her? What if her mom hated her so much, she didn't even want to know where she was or if she was okay? As long as she stayed out of touch, Emerson could pretend her mother missed her a tiny bit.

Emerson had run because she'd felt unwanted. If she called and felt that way all over again, then what? There was nowhere else to go. She'd be forced to carry that miserable feeling with her until the end.

It seems like the only logical thing to do is to keep putting it off. "Maybe tomorrow."

"Just remember, tonight's the last night you can say that."

"Okay, Mr. Stating-the-Obvious, I'll remember that."

He laughs. "You and your ridiculous names."

"You love them and you know it."

"You're right. I do. I'm going to miss them."

It stops her in her tracks. "Don't say that," she whispers.

"Say what?"

She rubs her temples and stares out at the empty street. "That you're going to miss me. Or something about me. Like, we won't be together . . . afterward."

He doesn't say anything. Just reaches up and pulls her hand down and takes it. Holds it tightly, trying to reassure her.

They keep walking. They're almost to the crosswalk that will take them to the park when a big guy with a shaved head steps out from the shadows of a building. It makes Emerson jump. Vince gets between her and the guy.

"We don't want any trouble," Vince says.

"Hey, take it easy," the guy says, putting his hands in the air. "No trouble here, trust me." He waves at the building behind him. "There's a party going on, if you're interested. No one over twenty-five allowed. Through the door and up the stairs, number 209. Got everything you could possibly want, if you know what I mean. I'm just running out to try and find more booze. Go on in if you'd like."

He takes off, jogging down the street, leaving them standing there, looking at the door to the building.

Emerson nudges Vince. "You should go. I can tell you want to."

"You don't?" he asks her.

"No."

"Nothing you want to do? Nothing you'd regret . . . not doing?"

She knows what he means, even if he doesn't say it. "Vince, I don't want my first time to be with a stranger. Maybe it's hard for you to understand, since it's different for guys. At least, that's what I've heard."

"Yeah." And that's all he says. He stands there a long time, looking at her.

"What?" she asks, nudging him again, trying not to get annoyed. "I'm sorry I don't want to go. But it's fine if you want to. I can meet up with you later. I mean, whatever you want to do. I don't want to hold you back."

"Em, I don't want to go without you," he says. "Don't you get it? I don't want anyone but you."

A shiver goes down her spine, even though it's not the least bit cool outside. She bites her lip. "I, uh—"

Although it's dark, there's just enough light from the streetlamps to see that he means what he says. His eyes are full of warmth and kindness.

Maybe more than that.

Wait. Definitely more than that.

The question is, does she feel the same way? Although, maybe at this point, it doesn't really matter.

For the first time, she's not thinking *no*. She's not telling herself she can't let it happen because she can't ruin things between them. Instead, she's thinking *maybe*. She's wondering, *Why not?*

*Why the hell not?*

Confused, she shakes her head just slightly, but he takes it the wrong way.

"Forget it," he says as he turns to go. "Come on."

She doesn't say anything more. Just follows him. Like always.

**THE FIRST** time
Emerson saw Vince,
he was standing on a corner,
playing a guitar,
singing the words
to a sad, sad song.

People rushed by
too busy for empathy.
What a sad, sad world.

She stood back,
listening,
and when he was done,
she walked up
and put a quarter
in his case.

He seemed insulted.

"Sorry," she muttered.
"I didn't leave home with much.

But you're good.
Really good."

He smiled at her.
The first smile
intended just for her
in a long, long time.

"You like to sing?" he asked.

She nodded.

And with that,
he started playing
and they sang together,
a happier song this time.

So happy together.

Until his guitar got stolen
a week later.

That's when Emerson
realized
living on the streets
is basically
one sad, sad song
after another.

# 12:30 a.m.

CARL AND Jerry ate a dozen or so stale pastries between the two of them and emptied an entire pot of decaffeinated coffee.

As they ate and drank, they shared their happiest memories. The best food they'd eaten. The best books they'd read. The best trips they'd taken.

Jerry has only been on one real trip his entire life. "There's just so much to see in Oregon," he'd explained. "Every time Mona and I talked about going somewhere else, we decided we should spend the time exploring the state we love the most."

"So where'd you go? When you finally did leave, I mean?"

"Alaska," he'd said with a smile. "We went to Alaska. For an entire month. Had the time of our lives sightseeing and, then, fishing for a week. Sent home coolers full of salmon that we ate all year long."

He sounded like a poet as he described it.

Towering glaciers. Majestic wilderness. Glistening waters.

As he'd shared more and more about the trip, Carl found himself wishing he could go to Alaska. He'd been to lots of places. Hawaii. Mexico. Even Italy.

But never Alaska.

*Why not?* he wondered, feeling a deep pang of regret.

He hated that feeling. It was the one thing he'd wanted to avoid at all possible costs.

"I shouldn't be so sleepy," Jerry says now. "But I am."

"Do you have a car? I could drive you home, if you'd like." Carl means it when he says it. But he's thinking about the possibilities, too. Maybe he could take Jerry home and then drive himself home. After all, Jerry probably wouldn't need the car for anything else.

"Yes. I have a car," Jerry says as he stands up. "But I think I'd like to rest here. Just for a little while. I'm so exhausted, I can hardly keep my eyes open."

Carl didn't tell him about trying to get home. He hadn't wanted to burden the old man with his problems. It didn't seem right.

"Okay," Carl says. "I'll nap a while, too."

"You don't have to. You can go, if you have somewhere to be. I'm sorry, I didn't even ask about your family."

"No. It's all right. My plan was to eat something, and then rest. I've been awake a long time."

And so, with that settled, Jerry heads for the door that leads to the kitchen. "There's a small room with a cot back here," he explains. "The napping room, my wife called it. She could catch a few winks in the early morning hours while waiting for a batch of goodies to bake."

While Jerry gets the napping room, Carl gets the cool, tiled floor. Before he lies down, he goes behind the counter and crumples up a bunch of paper bags to use as a pillow.

It's not the best, but it will do.

Carl goes to sleep thinking about fishing for salmon in Alaska. Regret is a hard thing to shake.

EMERSON TAKES a seat on a bench and looks out, past the streetlights, to the dark, dark water of the Willamette River. Vince sits next to her, his leg nervously bouncing up and down.

"Em?"

"Yeah?"

"I'm sorry. If I came across too strong. Or whatever. I shouldn't have said that."

"It's fine."

"Fine? What do you mean, fine?"

"I mean," she says, "it didn't bother me. So don't worry about it."

Vince is quiet for a moment. Then he says, "I can't help the way I feel."

"I know."

"And I guess you can't help the way you don't feel," he says softly.

"Vince—"

Before she can finish, a woman, decked out in running gear, approaches. She looks a little out of sorts.

"Hey," Vince says to her. "Everything okay?"

The woman scoffs. "Are you really asking me that right now?"

"Sorry," Vince says, like he really means it. "Stupid question. What I meant was, are you okay?"

"No. Not really. I came down here to go for a run at twilight. It's my favorite time of day to run. But when I went back to where I parked my car, it was gone. Someone stole it, I guess? I don't know. I'm not sure what to do. I found a bar that was open and sat there for a few hours, until things started getting weird. Now I'm trying to figure out what to do next."

It sort of surprises Emerson, how much this stranger shares with them. Hayden was the same way. Must have something to do with the fact that they are all in this weird waiting-for-the-sky-to-fall crisis together.

"Do you have family you can call?" Emerson asks as she stands.

"No. They're all on the East Coast. They wanted me to come back there, but, God, at the time, it seemed so extreme. I kept thinking something would happen. Someone would find a way to fix it. My life is here. It sounds so ridiculous now, but I had work to do. A shitload of work."

Now Vince stands. "So, you're not married?"

"It's such a cliché, but only to my career," she replies matter-of-factly. She crosses her arms and turns so she's looking out at the water. "Isn't it funny? The things we realize as the time gets shorter and shorter?"

"Yeah," Vince says. "That's for sure."

"I'm sorry," the woman says. "I should go. You two probably want to be alone."

"No," Vince says. "Actually, we'd like to try and help you. That's how we've decided to spend our last day. What's your name?"

She holds her hand out, like she's done this a million times. "I'm Jackie."

"Nice to meet you," Vince says, shaking her hand. "I'm Vince and this is Emerson."

Jackie reaches over and shakes Emerson's hand. "Can you tell us if there's anything you've been wishing for lately?" Emerson asks.

"Besides your car," Vince says. "If it's been stolen, I'm not sure we can help you with that."

"You'll think it's strange," Jackie says.

Emerson remembers how Hayden said almost the exact same thing. "Nah," Vince says. "We won't."

"I was supposed to go to Paris in October," she says. "And it's all I can think about. I've wanted to go there since I was a little girl, and just when I finally get the chance, it's snatched away from me." She shakes her head. Stares at the ground. "God, I sound like a bratty five-year-old, don't I?"

"Not at all. I get it. Come on," Vince says, turning back toward the city. "I know just the place to take you."

Emerson grabs his arm and he spins around. "Vince. You heard what she said, right? Paris. As in, France."

He smiles so big, his dimples show. "Yeah, I know. Let's go."

"OH MY God," Jackie says, pointing to a car on the street. "That's it. My car." She spins around, taking in their location a few blocks up from the waterfront. "I can't believe I did that. I thought I parked on Stark Street, but it's actually Oak Street. I wasn't paying much attention, I guess." She turns and looks at Emerson and Vince. "You two must think I'm a complete idiot."

"No, we don't," Vince says. "You got confused. It happens. The important thing is you found it. And now, if it's all right with you, we can drive and get there a hell of a lot faster."

"Where?" Jackie asks. "Where are we going, exactly?"

"You have to trust me, okay?" Vince says. He holds his hand out. "Can I have the keys? I'd like to drive. It'll be more of a surprise that way."

Emerson starts to protest. Because he doesn't even have a driver's license. In fact, she's not even sure he knows how to drive. But she doesn't say anything. Maybe right now, given the circumstances, it's not a big deal. If Vince wants to drive, if he's confident he can get them where they need to go, then she should trust him.

Jackie pulls the keys out of a pocket in her running pants and hands them to Vince as they walk across the street. When they get closer, Emerson can see it's a nice car. Like, a really nice car.

"Wow," Vince says, unlocking the doors, "I've never ridden in a BMW before."

"This was my gift to myself after I got promoted to vice president," she explains. "A new pair of shoes just wasn't going to cut it."

Jackie starts to step around to the passenger side, and then stops. She stares at Vince and Emerson, as they stand there with their hands on the door handles. Emerson can almost see the wheels turning in Jackie's brain.

"Maybe this isn't such a good idea," Jackie says. "I mean, I don't even know you. What if you're serial killers, out for a final thrill?"

Vince laughs his sweet, boyish laugh. Emerson points to his Charlie Brown shirt. "Do we honestly look like serial killers?"

Jackie considers this for a second as she runs her hand through her short dark hair. "You're right. You don't look like serial killers. So, what are you doing, exactly?"

"We're just trying to help people," Vince says. "That's all. Someone helped us earlier and told us to pay it forward. So, we are."

Jackie doesn't say anything more. She opens the door and gets into the passenger seat while Emerson gets in the back. Vince adjusts his seat, then puts the keys in the ignition and starts the car. Classical music blares out of the speakers. Jackie reaches for the stereo and turns it down.

"Sorry," she says. "I usually listen to alternative rock, but I thought maybe classical would be nice about now. Soothe my frazzled nerves or something like that."

"It's nice," Vince says as he puts the car into drive. "I like it."

"Lights would be good," Jackie says, reaching over and turning them on.

While Vince drives, Emerson thinks about this special talent Vince seems to have in coming up with ways to help these people make their wishes come true. When Jackie said, "Paris," Emerson couldn't think of a single thing they might be able to do for her. But Vince thought of something right away.

He's definitely one of the most empathetic people, if not the most empathetic person, she's ever known. She might not know much about his past, but she knows he's grown up with more than his fair share of pain and heartbreak. How does someone like that become the kind of person so few people are able to be?

Last Christmas, an old lady walked up to Emerson and Vince while they were panhandling, and handed each of them a baggie with a peanut-butter-and-jelly sandwich and a ten-dollar bill stuffed inside.

"Merry Christmas," she said. "I'll be praying for you."

"Thank you," Vince and Emerson told her.

Emerson slapped Vince on the shoulder once the lady was gone. "Dude, can you believe it? We're rich! What are you gonna get? I think I might buy myself some new underwear. And if there's money left over, a chicken sandwich from Mickey D's."

Vince fished the ten-dollar bill out of the baggie. "I'm gonna give it to Buzz. He can buy some cough medicine. Maybe a hot meal, too."

Buzz was an old guy they knew who'd been sick for weeks. Everyone kept telling him to go to the hospital, but he wouldn't do it. Emerson would never forget the look on Buzz's face when Vince handed him the money. Tears welled up in the old man's eyes and he said, "You sure you want to waste it on some good-for-nothing guy like me?"

Vince just smiled and said, "I'm sure. But you have to use it to help with that cough of yours."

"I will," Buzz said. "If I can just get some sleep, that'll help."

After they bought him some medicine, Vince went a step further and ran around the city, looking for a shelter that would take Buzz for a night or two. Once Vince found a place, he helped get Buzz there. A couple of weeks later, Buzz was as good as new.

It's like Vince was born to help people.

They head away from downtown and back toward northwest Portland, where they were earlier with Hayden. They could have walked if they'd had to, but Emerson is thankful for the ride. Her legs are tired. Actually, her whole body is tired. She doesn't want to give in to the fatigue, but as her eyelids grow heavy, she realizes resistance may be futile.

They have the streets to themselves, it seems. It's like a dream, driving through the night in a fancy car that smells like leather seats and floral perfume. A nice dream. Emerson sinks back and closes her eyes.

"We're here."

Vince's voice startles her, making her jump out of her seat.

"Were you sleeping, Em?" he asks after he opens her door.

"Uh, no. Maybe. I don't know. Anyway, let's go. I can't wait to see where you're taking us."

Vince leads Jackie and Emerson to the front door of a café. "Don't say anything yet. It may not look like much, but it's gonna be good. You'll see."

He tries the door, but it's locked. After a couple of knocks, Emerson turns around, thinking they can try the back door, when Vince says, "Wait. Someone's coming."

A moment later, a light comes on and a good-looking twentysomething guy with a scruffy face opens the door. "Can I help you?"

"Hey there. I was hoping we could maybe, uh, come in? Get something to eat?" Vince says. "I know it probably seems odd, but we have a good reason for coming here."

The guy yawns. Scratches his head. "Sure. Why not?" He steps aside and holds the door open for them.

The place is nice, with big glass cases that run practically wall to wall, and lots of quaint little tables and chairs.

"I haven't made anything new for a couple of days," the guy explains. "But you're welcome to have whatever's left."

Vince walks along the glass case until he seems to find what he was looking for. He turns and smiles. "Here we go. This is what I wanted. The macarons."

"Ah," the guy says. "Of course. There must be a fan of Paris among you."

Jackie sheepishly raises her hand. "That'd be me. I was supposed to go in October. I'm sort of heartbroken about it."

The guy genuinely looks sad for her. "I'm sorry. That's really terrible. That you won't get to go, I mean."

"Yeah, so, we thought we'd try and bring a little bit of Paris to her," Vince says.

"Are you sure it's okay?" Emerson asks. "I mean, we're not, like, interrupting anything, are we?"

The guy shakes his head. "Nah. I'm just hanging out here, since there's nowhere else I'd rather be. My friends all left. My family's back East, and I didn't go when I should have. I'm kind of embarrassed to say it, but I was a complete skeptic about the whole thing."

Emerson looks at Jackie, since this story sounds very familiar. Jackie doesn't take her eyes off him as she says, "Hey. Me too. Sucks, doesn't it?"

He sighs. "Yeah." Scratches his head again. "I'm Phillipe, by the way."

"Nice to meet you, Phillipe," Jackie says, stepping forward. Phillipe takes her outstretched hand and shakes it. It seems to Emerson that it lasts maybe a second longer than a handshake normally does.

"The name Phillipe sounds French," Emerson says. "Is it? I mean, do you happen to be French?"

"Part, yes." Then, in a charming French accent, he says, "But tonight, I shall be one hundred percent French, *oui*?" He moves toward a table. "Madame, would you like to take a seat?"

"Mademoiselle," Emerson corrects. "She's not married."

Phillipe smiles. "Ah. Very well." He pulls a chair out. "Please, sit. And I shall do my best to make this a night in Paris you shall never forget."

*THE THREE* take a seat
and the lights are dimmed.

From behind the counter,
music plays.

Sultry sax, soft drums,
and the sweet sound of a piano.

And then, a woman sings.
It's a familiar song, even in French,

one of romance, of love,
and of all things that are good.

Like magic, they are there,
in the City of Light

with the Eiffel Tower
looming large as people

walk cobblestone streets,
eating bread and kissing cheeks.

Tables and chairs are pushed aside,
leaving plenty of space.

Phillipe smiles and
holds out his hand.

Jackie stands and steps
into his welcoming arms.

They glide across the café floor,
starry-eyed, and the mood is contagious.

Vince takes Emerson's hand
and leads her to a corner.

He whispers in her ear as
he takes her in his arms.

"Welcome to Paris,
*ma chérie.*"

CARL DREAMS of their wedding day.

It was a small affair, with their closest friends and family members. They'd found a little country church on the top of a hill in the middle of nowhere, surrounded by fields of green.

"It's perfect," Trinity had said when they'd driven up to it. "I don't even have to look inside. This is it."

And so it was.

They wed on a sunny July day, with blue skies outside and pink zinnias inside. When she walked down the aisle, Carl was certain he'd never seen anyone more beautiful. It wasn't her wedding dress, necessarily. After all, she'd gone with a very basic design. It was simply seeing her there, coming toward him with that lovely smile of hers, ready to commit to being his partner for life.

After they said their vows, exchanged rings, and kissed, they turned and made their way outside while the small organ played.

The reception was held at a nearby winery, where they ate and drank and danced until the clock struck ten. And then, it was time to go. They had a plane to catch to Maui.

"That was so much fun," she said once they were in the backseat of the hired town car and on their way. "Thank you."

She kissed him.

"We're going to be happy," he told her. "I promise."

She smiled. She tried to hide it. But a tear slipped out.

There was nothing for him to say except, "I'm sorry. I'm so sorry."

"I know," is all she said.

She leaned into him and he wrapped his arms around her. And they never discussed it again.

Her parents hadn't approved of their marriage. He wasn't what they'd wanted for their daughter. He didn't come from a family of wealth or importance. After all, his father owned a landscaping business.

They'd met in college, where Carl had been accepted into the Master Gardener program, so he could help his father with the family business. Trinity was there to study fashion design. Her parents would have chosen someplace better for their daughter. But she insisted on going to Oregon State University. Corvallis, Oregon, was very different from Santa Monica, where she'd grown up, and she desperately wanted something different.

But, for the wedding, there was no denying it. She'd wanted them there. And they hadn't come.

For years after that, she only spoke to her parents on holidays and birthdays. They never came to visit. Once every few years, she would make the trip to see them. Alone.

And so it was, when the horrible news hit.

"I should go to them," she said. "I'm their only child."

Carl had wanted to say, "And I'm your only husband." But he didn't. Instead, he said, "I understand. Do what you have to do."

They said their good-byes as if she wouldn't be coming back.

Now Carl sits up straight, pulled from his dreams and back to the reality that confronts him.

She came back. And now he has to get home.

THEY EAT pink, yellow, and purple French macarons—the sweet, nutty cookies that are crunchy on the outside and creamy on the inside. So divinely delicious, Emerson can't imagine how she's lived her whole life and never eaten one.

As they drink tea out of old-fashioned teacups with dainty flowers painted on them, they talk and laugh like old friends. Here, in the cozy café with tea and cookies and sweet, adoring music, there is no sadness. No regret. No worries.

Only joy.

It's strange how quickly it happens, and yet, at the same time, slowly, too. Emerson can't help but notice the glances. The tenderness in their eyes. And the longing.

Phillipe and Jackie take another twirl around the café-turned-dance-floor and Emerson leans in and whispers to Vince, "I'm thinking we should go."

"How come?"

"Look at them. They haven't been able to take their eyes off each other."

They both watch for a moment and then Vince turns to Emerson and says, "Okay. But one more dance first." She eyes him curiously. "Please?" he begs.

So, she stands up and he does the same. He holds his hands out and she puts one hand on his shoulder and the other one in his hand. There is space between them for a moment, but he pulls her closer, until her head is practically resting on his chest.

"You're so tall," she says, looking up at him.

"No, you're just short."

The soft, jazzy music plays and they move ever-so-slowly.

"Where'd you learn to dance anyway?" Emerson teases. "A cute girl teach you?"

His eyes turn cold and he stares straight ahead. "No. Nothing like that. If you have to know, it was my mom."

Emerson reaches up and touches his nose playfully. "Hey, don't get mad. I didn't know."

He talks as they sway back and forth, his features softening as he does. "I can still picture it. Our little kitchen that smelled like everything good in this world. The sink where she washed the dishes. The window that looked out at the backyard. The old white refrigerator where she hung my artwork from school. She always cooked with the radio blaring. And every once in a while, she'd grab me and make me dance with her." He shakes his head. "Man, I thought she was ridiculous at the time. But now . . ."

His voice trails off.

Emerson doesn't say anything. Just presses in closer, hoping he knows that she understands. Knows how that painful feeling of missing comes in waves. You just have to ride it out. Brace yourself and let it wash over you, wincing as it does, until it eventually subsides. It can only pull you under if you let it.

Neither of them says anything for a while. Emerson can't deny it: She likes this. Likes the ambience. The music. The closeness. She feels safe in a way she hasn't felt in a long, long time.

"Em?" he says softly.

She looks up at him again. "Yeah?"

He doesn't respond right away, and Emerson's heart speeds up as she wonders if this is where it will finally end. If she'll finally stop fighting and let things spiral in a new direction, like a top on a table, moving closer and closer to the edge.

It's both exhilarating and terrifying.

He tucks a strand of her hair behind her ear. Touches her cheek just slightly. And then he finally says, "Thanks for being my best friend."

She swallows hard as she realizes in that moment that nothing is going to change unless she speaks up. Vince will remain the loyal and faithful friend she's wanted—no, *needed*, until the very end, unless she tells him her feelings have changed.

Because they have. Haven't they?

How can she be sure?

She wants to be sure.

For now, she looks into his warm and caring eyes and says, "Stop it. You know I don't like that sentimental crap."

He gives her a lopsided grin. "Actually, girl, I think you kind of love it."

She shakes her head in indignation as she moves in close to him again. He knows her too well.

"I THINK we're gonna go," Emerson says as the song ends and Phillipe and Jackie linger in each other's arms.

"Oh," Jackie says, stepping away from her dance partner and toward Emerson and Vince. "Are you sure? I mean, I think it's okay if we stay." She looks at Phillipe. "Right?"

"Absolutely," he says. "You're welcome to stay as long as you'd like."

"Jackie, you should definitely stay," Vince says. "But we have some stuff we want to do." He goes over to Phillipe and shakes his hand. "Thanks for everything, man."

"Yeah," Emerson says, rubbing her hands together nervously. "This was great. Thank you."

Phillipe goes to Jackie and puts his arm around her. Willing her to stay, Emerson thinks. And she should. It's like they belong together.

Jackie turns and looks at Phillipe. He smiles. She turns back and says, "Okay. Well, it was great meeting you guys. I mean, really great. This was so . . . perfect."

"It was," Emerson says as she walks over and gives Jackie a hug. In her ear Emerson whispers, "And he's perfect for you."

And then, they're heading toward the door. Leaving Paris for the great unknown. Emerson is surprised at how hard it is to go. She likes it here, where there's tea and cookies and lovely music. But she knows it's important they leave the two of them alone. There is only so much time, after all.

" 'Bye," Vince says, giving a little wave.

"You should take my car," Jackie says. "You still have the keys, right? Take it. Go somewhere fun."

Emerson shakes her head in disbelief. "Are you sure? I mean, what if you want to go somewhere?"

"I have a car," Phillipe says. "I can take her anywhere she wants to go."

It's settled, then. They are now the proud owners of a BMW. And with it comes a kind of freedom neither of them has had for a really long time.

"Thanks, Jackie," Emerson says.

"No," she says. "Thank you. Running into you guys tonight was the best thing that could have happened to me."

And then there's nothing left to say. Except good-bye, which Emerson can't quite get out. Apparently, Paris is a hard place to leave. So she just waves and walks through the door quickly.

She wraps her arms around herself as the cool night air brushes her skin.

"You okay?" Vince asks as he fishes the keys out of his pocket.

"I think so."

"Hard to leave?"

"That place was enchanting," she says. "You're really good at this thing we're doing. This Make-a-Wish-for-the-Apocalypse, or whatever you want to call it."

Vince laughs. "Make-a-Wish-for-the-Apocalypse? You have such a way with words, Em."

She walks around to the passenger side. "And *you* have a way with making wishes come true. Are you secretly a fairy godmother or something?"

They get into the car. "That's it. You've found me out," Vince says as he puts the key in the ignition.

"Well, don't worry. Your secret's safe with me. But seriously, come on. You couldn't have picked a better place to give Jackie a taste of Paris."

"Yeah, the mood was pretty unbelievable."

Emerson shakes her head. "And on top of that, she found romance, which is what everyone wants when they go to Paris."

Vince doesn't say anything for a moment. Just stares at Emerson. "Is that right?" he finally says.

Emerson gives Vince's leg a little shove. "Well, unless you're a doofus wearing a Charlie Brown T-shirt."

"I'm sorry," he says, settling back in his seat and turning the key. "My fairy godmother dress is at the cleaner's."

She smiles. "I'm sure it is. So, where are we going now?"

"How about the library?" Vince asks. "You said you wanted to look at books, and I'm dying to find out the name of that kid in the *Peanuts* gang. Like, you wouldn't believe how much it's bugging me that we can't remember his name. What do you say?"

Emerson chuckles. "Sure. Fine. It's not like I have anything better to do, right?"

**WINDOWS ROLLED** down.
Cool breeze in their hair.
Bare feet on the dash.

It could be the
perfect summer night
if not for the fact that
doomsday is now
officially here.

There's one radio station
still playing tunes.

Vince turns it up,
because this song
demands to be heard.

They sing at the top
of their lungs
along with good old
Tom Petty.

The wai-ai-ting
is the
har-dest

part.

THE NIGHT has gone from warm and friendly to sad and lonely. Carl sits on the floor of the napping room, weeping.

He's dead. Jerry is dead. Carl tried to wake him, to let him know he had to be going, and that it was such a pleasure to meet him. But Jerry didn't move.

He jumped back at the realization of what had happened, and then sank to the floor, his head in his hands.

Carl knows he should be happy for the old man. And maybe, deep down, he is. After all, Jerry died peacefully, while sleeping, in a place where he felt close to his wife. Unlike the rest of them, Jerry doesn't have to sit in fear of what will happen later.

In so many ways, Jerry is better off. Carl knows this, and yet he can't stop crying. Perhaps it's not about the old man as much as it is about himself.

He doesn't want to die. He thought he did, earlier, and thought it would be easier to help things along. But now, as he stares at the old man, so still and quiet, it hits him—what it all really means.

He'll miss the sound of rain on the rooftop.

The smell of cookies baking in the oven.

The warmth of sunshine on his skin.

The beating of his heart in that dreamy, tender moment before his lips meet Trinity's.

Her touch. Her lips.

Her.

So many moments he took for granted, and suddenly, he wants to experience them all, again and again, a thousand times at least.

If only he could stop crying. Could get up and move and find a way home.

But there is death in the room. And death makes you feel sad in a way that nothing else does.

How can something inevitable be so hard to accept?

"I'm sorry," Carl whispers.

For Jerry.

For Trinity.

And for everyone who must live today worrying about what's to come.

"WOW," VINCE says as he pulls on one of the doors that lead to the Multnomah County Library. "It's open."

"You know what they say," Emerson tells him as she walks through the door he holds for her. "Knowledge is forever."

Someone even left some lights on here and there, too. They walk through the lobby, and although Emerson expects to see other people, no one is around.

"Hey, Vince, why do you think we still have electricity? It's kind of weird, isn't it? Did you read anything about that? In the newspaper, I mean?"

"Nope. Who knows what's going on? Maybe they're keeping it on to make things a little less scary for everyone."

"Hm. Maybe."

Emerson heads toward the children's section and Vince follows. When they find the comics and graphic novels for kids, Vince starts scanning the shelves.

"I'll be over in the picture books," Emerson tells him. "Come and find me when you're done."

"Got it."

As she immerses herself in the picture book stacks, the slightly musty smell of old books transports Emerson back to the days when her mom took the girls to the city library every other week during summer vacation. Afterward, they'd stop for ice cream cones at the Dairy Queen. Emerson rotated through the flavors of ice cream and dipped coatings, because she loved trying the different combinations. Chocolate ice cream dipped in cherry. Vanilla ice cream dipped in butterscotch. And her favorite, twist ice cream dipped in chocolate. Her mother used to get so mad as Emerson tried to figure out which combination to order.

"Hurry up and decide," she'd screech as they sat in their car at the drive-through menu. "There's a line behind us."

Her sister, on the other hand, got the same cone every time—vanilla ice cream dipped in cherry. That was the thing about Frankie. She never caused problems. She was the easy child—the one you could count on to do the right thing all the time.

Emerson had often longed to be more like her sister, but whenever she tried, she grew bored within ten minutes. There seemed to be a need, deep inside of her, to shake things up as often as possible. Before her mom had kicked her out, Emerson had ignored her curfew again and again. If she got grounded, she simply snuck out once everyone else had fallen asleep.

After all, there were parties to go to. Cemeteries to play in. Hikes to go on in the dark, without a flashlight. Fear, excitement, elation—she wanted to feel it all. Every time she went out with her friends, they tried their best to push the fun factor up a notch or two. They always wanted more.

For Emerson, life was about trying every flavor of cone possible. Doing the easy thing, the right thing, just didn't seem to be in her DNA.

When her mom told her she had to go live with her dad, Emerson had cursed her fun-seeking DNA. If only she'd tried harder to be more like her sister.

Now she searches the shelves for the one book she suddenly wants to find. As she looks, she runs across many childhood favorites—*The Very Hungry Caterpillar*, *Mike Mulligan and His Steam Shovel*, and *Click, Clack, Moo: Cows That Type*.

And then, there it is. The one she's been looking for. She runs her hand across the red cover and smiles down at the adorable little bear.

Corduroy. The bear who wants, more than anything, to find a home.

She turns the page and begins to read when Vince startles her. "Franklin," he says, standing over where she's sitting on the floor. "The black kid's name is Franklin."

Emerson nods. "That's right. Now I remember. Glad we won't lose any more sleep over that one."

Vince plops down next to her. "What'd you find?"

"One of my favorite books."

"Will you read it to me?" he asks with his impossible-to-resist lopsided grin. "Pretty please?"

"I'd love to," she says.

And so, she reads the story, slowly, taking lots of time for them to admire the illustrations. When she gets to the end, and Corduroy finds a home, Emerson's voice catches in her throat.

"Hey," Vince says, putting his fingers under her chin and turning her head to look at him. "What's wrong?"

She swallows hard. "I just wish I could go home."

"Then what are we doing? Let's go. We have a car, remember?"

Emerson shakes her head. "No. It's not that easy."

"The hell it isn't."

She reaches over and, very carefully, like there's a real live bear in between the pages, puts the book back in its spot. "It's not about going home," she tries to explain. "It's not about the place, you know? It's about the feeling. The feeling of being home, with people who want you there. That's what I want." She waves her hand at the bookcase. "What Corduroy wanted." She stands up. "You get what I mean."

Vince stands, too. "You're right. I do. But, Em, things have changed. You haven't been home in a long time, and with everything that's happened, I'm telling you, I really think she'll be happy to see you."

She shakes her head again, because it seems completely absurd to even imagine a happy reunion.

"No," is all she says.

"You won't know unless you try."

It's true. She won't. But she also won't have the door slammed in her face.

"You know that saying, 'Ignorance is bliss'?" she asks him.

"Yes."

"Well, sometimes ignorance is also necessary for one's sanity. And since it's one of the few things I have in my possession at the moment, I'm not quite ready to give that up."

BEFORE VINCE can say anything else, a woman and a little girl approach them. It seems odd to see them there, even though it shouldn't be. It's a public library, after all. Still, Emerson stares at them, wondering what they could possibly be doing here, in the middle of the night. The little girl should be in bed, sound asleep.

"My apologies," the petite woman says, with an East Indian accent. "We don't mean to interrupt."

"You're not," Vince says. "We just finished reading *Corduroy*. It's a good book, if you're looking for something to read."

"We were asleep, in the corner," the woman says matter-of-factly.

"Oh no, we woke you up, didn't we? I'm sorry," Emerson says, because she means it. "We didn't know anyone was here."

"It's okay," the girl says. "I'm not tired anymore."

"It probably seems strange, that we'd be sleeping here, but we left home a couple of days ago and didn't really have anywhere to go," the woman explains. "We're just sort of . . . waiting."

"Waiting until Papa leaves, and then we can go home again," the girl says. "He was getting really mad about everything, so we left. Mama said he needed some time alone. But hopefully we can go back the day after tomorrow."

Emerson looks at the woman and she can see the pleading in her eyes. The girl doesn't know. She's clueless about what's going to happen soon. Her mother has somehow managed to keep it a secret from her.

"He's not handling things well right now," the woman explains. "It's harder for some people than others, yes? But soon things will be back to normal. Soon everything will be fixed. I'm sure of it."

"Right," is all Vince says.

"I should introduce ourselves," the woman says. "I'm Rima and this is Inika."

"I'm Vince, and this is my friend Emerson."

"It is our pleasure to meet you," Rima says.

"How old are you, Inika?" Emerson asks.

"Six," she replies.

Emerson turns and looks at Vince, wondering if he's going to offer to do something for them. She feels sadness for these two in a way she didn't feel with the others. Probably because of the little girl, she decides. There's so much Inika hasn't done yet. So much she'll miss out on.

Vince kneels down in front of the young girl. "I'm wondering, what do you want to be when you grow up? If you could be anything, what would it be?"

"That's easy," Inika replies. "I want to be a vet. You know, an animal doctor. Mama says I can be anything I want to be." She looks up at her mother with her beautiful brown eyes. "Isn't that right?"

"That is correct," Rima replies as she strokes her daughter's silky black hair.

Vince smiles. "You love animals, then?"

"Yes, I love them so much. My papa never let me have one,

but I've always wanted to have a kitty. I even have a name picked out."

"You do?" Vince asked. "What's the name?"

"Simba," Inika says. "Like in the movie."

"I love that name," Emerson says. "*The Lion King* was one of my favorite movies when I was little. Hey, I have an idea. How would you like to go and see a bunch of kitties? I know you're not allowed to take one home, but I bet you could stay and play with them as long as you wanted."

Inika's eyes grow big and round. "Really?" She looks at her mother. "Can we, Mama? Please?"

Vince leans in and whispers in Emerson's ear, "The animal shelter?"

Emerson nods as she talks to Rima. "See, we're doing this thing where we help people make their wishes come true. Someone did it for us, and so we've decided to do it for other people, too. It's been a lot of fun."

"I don't think so," Rima says, her brow furrowed. "We like it here. It's safe. Quiet."

"But, Mama, I want to see the kitties," Inika says. "Please? I won't ask to take one home, I promise."

"No," she says, more firmly this time. "It's the middle of the night and the kitties are asleep. Now, come along. Let's go use the restroom and then it's back to sleep for us as well."

Inika starts to cry, and it's like a stab to Emerson's chest.

"See? You're tired." Rima grabs her daughter's hand as she says, "Good luck to both of you." And then she hurries off, practically dragging Inika behind her.

"Oh my God," Emerson says. "I'm the worst person in the world. I broke that poor girl's heart."

"No," Vince says, shaking his head. "You didn't break her heart. Her mother did."

"But if I hadn't mentioned—"

"Come on," he says as he turns around. "Don't waste another minute worrying about it. If she wants to be safe, which is so ironic right now it's not even funny, then let her. There are plenty of other people out there who will be thrilled to let us help them."

Emerson follows him toward the door. But she can't shake the funny feeling in her stomach. Like she's done something terribly, terribly wrong.

*"I HATE* him."

Him being Kenny,
her mother's boyfriend.

After she said
those three little words,
they hung there,
forming a noose that
eventually ended
Emerson's life
as she knew it.

But she couldn't
do it anymore.
Couldn't pretend
that everything was
fine when it wasn't.

She thought Kenny was rude
and arrogant.

He thought Emerson was
obnoxious and selfish.

Not everyone
likes the same books,
the same movies,
the same foods.

And so it is
with people.

She couldn't make
herself like him
any more than she
could make herself
like *The Catcher in the Rye*.

The struggle
between mothers and daughters
was something Emerson
knew all too well.

But as she thinks
about Inika, and
Rima's seemingly
coldhearted ways,
she realizes one thing.

In the end,
it's Rima and her daughter,
together.

Not everyone
is so lucky.

EVENTUALLY, CARL pulls himself together. Under normal circumstances, he'd make calls. Or at least one call, to the police, letting them know someone has died.

But these aren't normal circumstances. Besides, the phone lines aren't even working. So although it seems completely wrong, there's really nothing to do but leave.

First, though, he reaches into Jerry's pocket and retrieves his key chain.

"Thank you," Carl whispers, as if Jerry's simply sleeping and he doesn't want to wake him.

Carl makes his way through the bakery and out the front door. Once outside, he leans against the front door and lets out the breath he didn't realize he'd been holding. He takes a minute to compose himself, then turns and locks the front door. Jerry had used a key his wife still had for the bakery. Carl hopes that by locking it up tight, no one will try to get in.

*Rest in peace, Jerry.*

With that done, he turns and scans the street, looking for Jerry's car. There are only two choices: a Subaru wagon on this side of the street and a Chrysler sedan on the other.

A streetlamp gives off just enough light for him to check the keys. There's a remote lock with the Chrysler logo on it.

He almost can't believe his luck. Thanks to Jerry, he now has a car. A way to get back.

In twenty minutes, he'll be home.

Home.

With Trinity.

The woman he loves.

They'll have an entire day together, and although it's not much, it's more than what he'd previously thought they'd have.

He crosses the street, unlocking the car with the remote as he goes. It beeps, letting him know it's worked. The doors are open.

He smiles.

Just as he's about to reach for the car door handle, there is an intense pain in his head. He doesn't have time to think, to try to figure out what it could be, to comprehend the fact that someone has hit him in the head from behind with something very, very hard.

He falls to the ground, dropping the keys as he goes.

VINCE IS driving. Hasn't said where they're going. Emerson kind of wonders, but she doesn't ask. Instead, she stays lost in her thoughts.

Of the past.

Of all the things that went wrong.

Of home. Or, what used to be home.

"What if they're wrong?" Vince asks, snapping Emerson back to reality.

"Who?"

"The so-called experts. What if it doesn't happen later today like they think? Or they find a way to prevent it? What if everything is going to be okay after all?"

"Vince, maybe you like pretending you're a fairy god-mother, but in reality, this is not a freaking fairy tale." She leans her head back and closes her eyes before she says in a soft voice, "I'm sorry, but I don't think we should delude ourselves."

"It's just, the way that lady talked. Rima. She sounded so sure."

"Because it's what she wants to believe. Doesn't mean she's right, you know?"

"Yeah. I guess."

Emerson looks out the window. They're somewhere in the West Hills. The road is dark, with lots of curves. Vince is driving slowly, though they haven't passed a single car. She decides to ask now. "So, you want to tell me where we're headed?"

"Nope. It's a surprise."

"Cool. I like surprises."

"I know. We talked about this once before, remember?"

"Right. You don't like surprises," Emerson says, recalling the conversation. "In fact, you dislike them so much, you read the end of the book first. You're the guy authors love to hate."

"Nah. I don't think that's true. They just want readers. It doesn't matter how they read. At least, it shouldn't."

"Well, I don't get it," Emerson says. "What's the point of reading the book, then?"

"There's more to a book than the ending, right? Just ask my old English teacher, Mr. Weir. He'd tell you there's way more. Like, the setting, the characters, and the obstacles those characters face."

Emerson sighs. "Sorry. I still don't get it."

"What about the asteroid?" Vince asks. "Would you have rather not known? Been surprised?"

"Definitely."

"Girl, not me. I'm glad we know. Look at all the fun we're having because we know."

"Yeah, but that's not all there is. There's also fear. Grief." She pauses. "Regret."

Vince is quiet for a moment. Then he asks, "Do you regret leaving home?"

Emerson leans her head on the cool glass window. "Maybe a little bit. I don't know."

"The thing is, Em, regret is not really helpful right now. Because you can't go back in time and change things. So why think that way?"

"Maybe because my brain is a big, sloppy mess, knowing we are going to *die* soon?"

Vince laughs. "Okay, okay. So maybe a little bit of that is normal." He glances at her briefly. "But can you try to remember the happy times?"

"Like the time I dove in that dumpster behind Rose's Deli and found not one, but two perfectly good cinnamon rolls? And then, on the way out, I found a needle someone had thrown in there and I was scared to death for days it had pricked me and I'd die of AIDS? Yeah, we've had some good times all right, Vince."

"You gotta admit, those cinnamon rolls were sweet."

Emerson smiles at the pun. "Yep. Sweet."

It's quiet for a few minutes. Then Vince says, "I don't regret any of it. Not one minute I spent with you. You know why?"

"No."

"Because you gave me a reason to get up every morning. A reason to fight to stay alive. Because some days, we had to fight hard."

"Harder than a mother-trucking prizefighter."

"But it was easier, with you there. It was easier, because we were together. You get that, don't you?"

"Yes," she whispers.

He reaches over and sets his hand on hers. He gently squeezes it, and then lets go. Part of her, the part that's said no for so long, is glad. But the other part of her, the part that keeps screaming at her that it doesn't matter anymore, is sad.

Now, more than ever, she wants someone to touch her. To hold her and protect her.

To love her.

But if she lets him in like that, it just seems like it will hurt even more. Like, hurt in a whole new way to have to say good-bye. And she's not sure she can handle any more pain right now.

Maybe Rima had it right, after all. Maybe it's easier, better even, to play it nice and safe.

"WHERE IS it?" Vince mutters, breaking the silence.

Emerson sits up straight, looking out the front window. They're passing some really nice houses. "If you tell me where we're going, maybe I can help."

"Ah, here we go," he says as he turns right. "Good. The gate's open."

"I'm curious," she says. "Had you even driven a car before tonight?"

"You know, I think that qualifies as one of those it's-best-to-leave-the-past-in-the-past questions."

She turns and stares at him. "Are you serious right now? I'm asking about your driving skills, not whether you were abused as a child."

He veers over to the side of the road and slams on the brakes. The seat belt tightens up around Emerson and, for a second, she can't breathe as the force of the stop pushes her forward while the seat belt holds her back.

"Whoa," she says. "What are you—"

He doesn't let her finish. When he turns and looks at her, the dashboard lights are bright enough for her to see his eyes. He looks like a soldier at war. Fierce. Powerful. And a little bit dangerous. "Don't ever joke about it, Emerson. Ever. You hear me?"

"Okay, okay. I hear you. I'm sorry." She bites her lip as she tries to figure out what she can do to calm him down. "It was a mistake, and you're right. I shouldn't joke about that."

He takes a deep breath and relaxes a little bit, leaning back in his seat. Emerson isn't sure she should say anything else, so she waits.

Finally, he talks, his voice softer now. "I had this one foster mom who taught me how to drive when I was fourteen. The one I lived with before I ran. Once I knew how, she used to make me drive her around at night. She had trouble sleeping, so she'd crawl in the back of her beat-up Ford Escort, with a fifth of tequila, and I'd drive until she fell asleep. That's how I got to know the Portland area so well."

She has more questions she wants to ask him. *Were there other kids in this woman's care? If so, what'd they do while you drove Mother Tequila around the city? Once you got home, how'd you get her inside? Did it ever scare you to be driving without a license?*

But she doesn't ask. Because she knows that whatever she went through with her parents, it was nothing compared to what Vince went through in foster care. Even though he's told her very little, she knows this like she knows her own name. While there's a part of Vince that is kindhearted and strong, there's also a part that is sad and bitter. He just does a good job of hiding it most of the time. While she considers what he told her, she suspects this story is one of the more tame ones.

Which is exactly why he went ahead and told her.

"Vince, I don't know what to say. Except I'm sorry." And she really means it.

"I know," he says. "And I'm sorry for going off the rails." He looks at her. "Are we okay?"

"Yes. Of course. We're always okay. No matter what."

He nods and puts the car into drive again. "Good." They go up a slight hill and around a corner, to an empty parking lot. "We're here."

It's pitch-black, so Emerson can't see much. "Where is here, exactly?"

"Hold on a minute. You'll find out soon enough." Vince opens his door so the dome lights come on. Then he reaches over and pops open the glove box. "Can you see if there's a flashlight in there? I'll check the trunk."

Emerson digs around, but all she finds are napkins, a car manual, and receipts.

"Got it," Vince yells, walking back around to the open door, now carrying a small flashlight. "She has an emergency road kit back there. Smart lady."

Emerson gets out and they walk across the parking lot, the flashlight shining in front of them.

"I have to pee," Emerson says.

"Yeah, me too," Vince replies. "They have bathrooms up here. We'll see if they're open."

"And if they're not?"

"You know the answer to that. We'll improvise. Like we've done every day for the past year and a half."

"Stupid improvising," Emerson says as she crosses her arms and holds them tightly against her chest. The temperature's dropped and she's cold. "I just want to sit on a toilet and pee."

When they come to a small building on their left, Vince stops. He shines the flashlight up ahead and even though there are lots of bushes and trees, Emerson can see there's a huge house there.

"Pittock Mansion," Vince says before she has the chance to ask him once again where they are. "You've heard of it, right?"

"No. Do people live here?"

"Not anymore. A wealthy couple, the Pittocks obviously, had it built in the early nineteen hundreds. Years later, after they died, the city of Portland bought it and had it restored. It's been a famous Portland landmark ever since."

"Huh," Emerson says. "Are we going inside?"

"I don't know if we can get in. The house isn't actually why I brought you here."

"It isn't?"

"Nope."

"And that's all you're going to tell me?"

He gives her a little nudge with his elbow. "You love surprises, remember?" He turns toward the little building. "Come on. Let's see if we can get in to use the bathroom."

Vince tries the door, and thankfully, it's open. "It's like they knew we were coming," he says. "Left the gate open. The bathrooms are unlocked. Maybe we'll be able to get into the house, after all."

Emerson steps through the door that Vince is holding open. He shines the flashlight in so she can find the door marked WOMEN.

"Here," he says as he hands her the flashlight. "We can take turns, since we only have one light."

As she sets the flashlight on the sink, standing on end so the ceiling lights up, Emerson wonders what Vince has planned.

She's not even going to try to guess. Because she always seems to guess wrong.

**IT WAS** cold.

The kind of cold
that makes your
fingers and toes ache.

The kind of cold
that makes you want
to curl your hands
around a big mug
of hot chocolate
and never let go.

The kind of cold
that made her
think about giving up
and going home.

They shared a cup
of coffee at a café until
closing time.

The shelters were full.
Their options were limited.

"I have an idea," Vince told her.
"Stay here,
while I see what I can do."

He came back a long while later
with a big smile on his face.

"Come on."

"Where are we going?"

"It's a surprise."

She thought he'd found
room at a shelter,
or an all-night restaurant
that would allow them to sit there,
drinking nothing but water.

Instead,
he took her to a small
motel where he had a key
to a room with two double beds,
a small television set with cable,
and, most importantly,
warm, glorious, much-needed heat.

"How'd you do it?" she asked him.

He turned on the television
and plopped down on one of the beds.

He smiled at her.
"That's not the right thing to say
when you get a gift, Em."

She walked over and
sat down next to him.
Put her head on his shoulder.

"I love my surprise.
Thank you."

"You're welcome."

He never did tell her how he did it.
She decided maybe it was best
if she didn't know.

They had a fabulous night
of cleaning themselves up,
watching TV,
talking and laughing,
and, finally, sleeping.

The next morning, they got up early
and snagged spots at a shelter
until the cold snap passed.

They lived a life with
a lot of uncertainty.
But one thing was for sure.

Vince was good at surprises.

THERE'S SOME tugging.

Lifting.

A lot of grunting.

Carl feels it all, but his head hurts so much, he keeps his eyes closed and doesn't fight it. Whoever it is seems to be trying to help him.

At least, he hopes that's what's happening.

He tries to form the word. To say where he wants to go. Where he needs to go. He tries and tries to open his mouth and say, "Home."

But he can't do it.

A door slams. And then, another one.

They're moving.

*Where are we going?* he wants to ask.

But the words don't come. Only darkness.

VINCE AND Emerson walk around the outside of the mansion, looking in the windows, though it's hard to see much. Every time they come to a door, they try opening it, but the place is locked up tight.

As they peer into a large picture window, giving them a peek of a room filled with very old-fashioned wingback chairs and a sofa, along with a piano and a harp, Vince says, "Can you imagine living here?"

"It's like something out of a movie," Emerson says. "Like, I'm half expecting Elizabeth Bennet to walk out here any minute, dressed in a lovely white frock with ribbons in her hair, as she waits for Mr. Darcy to come calling on her."

"Who?" Vince asks as he moves to another window and puts his hands and face up to it.

"You're kidding, right?"

"No. Never heard of them."

"From the book *Pride and Prejudice*? By Jane Austen? You've heard of it, right?"

"No. Can't say I have."

Emerson is about to tell him she can no longer call him a friend, when someone behind them clears her throat. They both spin around, startled.

"I love the movie," the teen girl says. "The one with Keira Knightley and Matthew Macfadyen? It's my favorite, actually. Both of them are just so, so perfect in it."

"Right," Emerson says. "I agree. I watched it at a friend's house one time. As soon as it was over, I wanted to watch it again."

"I hope I'm not bothering you guys," the girl says. "I live nearby, and couldn't sleep. Thought I'd come and see if the house happened to be open. I take it that it's not?"

"Unfortunately, no," Vince says. "And you're not bothering us at all. I'm Vince, and this is Emerson."

"Nice to meet you. I'm Katsumi, but you can call me Kat. So what's the deal? You couldn't sleep, either?"

Emerson waves at Vince. "He brought me here for some sort of surprise. I'm not sure what it is yet. Wait. I bet you're in on it, aren't you? I know, you're the movie director and Keira and Matthew are getting dressed as we speak. There's going to be a sequel, right? And I get to be in the movie? What do I play? The maid? Cook, maybe?"

Kat chuckles. "Maid? No way. You get to be the beautiful girl-next-door who's just moved in. And you have your eye on Mr. Darcy."

Emerson's hand flies to her mouth. "Oh, but I can't do that to poor Lizzy Bennet. I mean, she's waited so long to find love. What is she, nineteen? Twenty? The poor thing, she's practically an old maid, complete with shriveled-up lady parts."

"Yikes," Vince mutters. "Poor Mr. Darcy. Shriveled-up lady parts are no fun, man. No fun at all."

"Exactly," Kat says. "Which is why you must rescue him, Emerson. Save the dear chap, won't you?"

"No," Emerson says, putting her hand on her forehead as if she's suffering. "I can't do it. I mustn't. Please, just let me be a servant and I'll serve the couple well."

Kat pauses, seeming to consider this. "All right. Come along, then. Let me show you to your quarters."

Emerson turns and gives Vince an amused look. He shrugs. "Cool. I'm game."

Vince flips the flashlight back on as they walk down some stairs and around to the side of the mansion. Kat picks up a large stick, points it, and says, "This way," and proceeds to lead them to a small building nearby.

She jiggles the knob, but it's locked.

"Oh well," Vince says. "I guess—"

But before he can finish his sentence, Kat jabs the stick into the window at the top of the door, shattering the pane of glass into hundreds of pieces that fall to the ground.

"Can I get a little light over here, please?"

Vince does as she asks. Kat reaches in carefully, turns the knob, and opens the door. Then she stands back and says, "After you."

STRAIGHT AHEAD, there are stairs that lead up to another level. To the right is a small sitting room with an old-fashioned brick fireplace and a few simple chairs. To the left is a small bedroom complete with a bed, covered in a white chenille bedspread. Emerson turns and goes into the sitting room. Vince sets the flashlight on the mantel, lighting up the room surprisingly well.

Kat smiles as she steps into the room. "It's been a while since I took the official tour, but I think this was where the chauffeur lived. Cute, right?"

"Very," Emerson says, eyeing Kat and not the house. She glances at Vince and wonders if he's thinking the same thing. The girl is adorable, with her perfectly round face and pretty red lips. Of course, she also seems a little bit crazy, breaking the window like that without seeming to give it a second thought.

"Think you could live here?" Kat asks.

Vince takes a seat in one of the chairs. "Well, it's all right, but the place could definitely use some new furniture. And a flat-screen. What do you think, Em?"

Emerson trails her hand along the mantel. "I like it. In the evening, when my duties are done, I could come here and curl up next to a cozy fire. Read a book or write letters."

Vince shakes his head. "What do you mean, write letters? No one writes letters anymore. Come on. Get a flat-screen. I hear they're pretty cheap at Costco."

Kat clicks her tongue. "Clearly, you're not familiar with the time period. There are no televisions yet. No Costcos to shop at. Instead, there's a garden, where you grow carrots and snap peas and tomatoes. And, yes, you write letters. Lots of letters, because people love letters more than they love food, I think."

"It's the only way to stay in touch," Emerson adds.

"He really needs to read the book," Kat says as she sits in a chair next to Vince.

"I know," Emerson sighs. "We were at the library earlier. If only I'd known."

"What were you doing at the library?" Kat asks.

Emerson crosses her arms, wondering how much she wants to tell this girl who is practically a stranger. "We did a little research. And I found my favorite childhood book."

"Which is?" Kat asks.

Emerson hesitates, but Vince doesn't seem to notice. "*Corduroy.* You know, the one about the bear who wanders around in the department store, looking for a button?"

"Oooh, I love that one," Kat says. Then she turns to Vince. "So, after that, you came here? Are the two of you trying to visit all of your favorite places or something?" She sits back and sighs, before he's even had a chance to respond. "How romantic."

Emerson feels herself getting a little bit annoyed by Kat and her game of twenty questions. Doesn't she realize she's getting personal and maybe they don't want to get personal?

Vince stands up. "Actually, we've been on a kind of quest."

Emerson shakes her head slightly. It's a knee-jerk reaction; she doesn't even think about it. Something tells her this girl is not someone they should try to help. But Vince just grins as if to say, *It's fine, don't worry.*

"A quest?" Kat asks as she jumps to her feet. "Oh, I love the sound of that. What are you searching for?"

"People we can help," Vince says. "We're trying to make as many wishes come true as we can. It beats sitting around doing nothing, waiting for the inevitable, you know?"

Kat smiles. "Really? Oh my God, that is the sweetest thing I've ever heard. Does that mean you want to make my wish come true?"

Vince stuffs his hands in the pockets of his scruffy old jeans. "Yeah. Sure. If we can. Why, is there something you've always wanted to do?"

"Yes," she says, nodding enthusiastically. Then she looks at Emerson. "But I'm not sure—I mean, you might not like it."

Emerson's stomach feels funny. The way Kat is looking at Emerson, she knows something weird is about to happen.

"What is it?" Vince asks. "Just tell us."

"First, I want to ask you," Kat says as she fiddles with a pearl ring she's wearing. "Are you guys, like, boyfriend and girlfriend?"

"We're friends," Vince says, glancing at Emerson. Does he see something in her eyes? she wonders. Does he notice how uncomfortable this room is right now? "Best friends."

Kat instantly relaxes, dropping her arms to her sides as she says, "Oh, good. What a relief. Because, well, I wouldn't want to cause any problems for you two."

Vince looks at Kat curiously. "I'm not following you."

Kat laughs nervously. "See, I've never been kissed. I know it's probably hard to believe, that I'm sixteen and never been kissed. Like the title of a bad movie or something. But it's true. My parents are really strict. Like, you can't even believe how strict. I never get to go anywhere. Do anything."

Emerson steps forward. "So, are you asking what I think you're asking?"

Kat doesn't look at her. She just keeps her eyes on Vince. "I was hoping that maybe, um, you could make my wish come true? You know . . . kiss me?"

EMERSON SCOFFS. "I don't think—"

"No, it's fine," Vince says, not letting her finish. "If that's what she really wants."

"But you don't even know her," Emerson says, trying not to sound too indignant.

"I don't think that really matters right now," he replies.

"Are you sure?" Kat says. "Because I don't want, like, a peck on the cheek or something. I want a real one." She smiles, trying to look sweet. But to Emerson, she looks absolutely evil. "A good one."

Emerson can't believe what she's hearing. Is this girl for real?

"Yeah," Vince says. "Okay. You want to do it in here, or outside, or what?"

"But what about my surprise?" Emerson says, stepping between them. "You haven't even showed me what it is yet."

Kat shrugs. "You can do that first. I don't mind."

"Actually," Vince says, "I can't. Not yet. It's not quite ready."

"Not ready?" Emerson asks. "I don't get it. Are you baking me a cake in that fancy house or something?"

Kat pushes into Emerson, leaning toward Vince. "Oh, I bet I know what it is. Your surprise. Is it—"

Vince reaches up and puts his hand over Kat's mouth. "No! Don't say it. I don't want to ruin it."

Kat takes Vince's hand and pulls it away from her mouth. As she brings it down, she doesn't let go. "Okay, okay. My lips are sealed. At least until we kiss." She chuckles. "Because that wouldn't be very fun."

"All right," Emerson says, stepping back, her hands raised. "You know what? I think I'll step outside so you guys can do your thing and get it over with. I'm tired of hearing you talk about it."

Kat nods as she looks at Vince. "We could maybe, I don't know, go into the bedroom?"

"Oh my God," Emerson says, glaring at Kat. "Are you serious right now?"

"Yeah," she replies. "I just think it'd be more comfortable in there. We can sit on the bed and be . . . close."

"Right," Vince says. Is that eagerness in his voice? Emerson isn't sure. "Fine with me."

*Stop it,* Emerson tells herself. *Stop being ridiculous. He can do whatever he wants. Let him kiss her and get it over with. Then she'll leave and you'll get your surprise, and everything will go back to normal.*

*Won't it?*

**HE TRIED** to kiss her once.

Emerson surprised Vince
with a new coat
she'd found at the skate park.
Someone had left it behind.

Probably wore it there,
then got hot and took it off
and forgot to grab it
when he went home.

It was nice.
Thick and warm,
with a hood.

When she gave it to him,
he was like a little kid
getting a Tonka toy on
Christmas morning.

It fit like it was
made for him.

"Thank you, Em," he said.
"It's perfect.
I love it."

"I'm glad," she said.

He looked at her,
and she just knew.
She knew what was coming next.
He got the words out quickly,
like they might get away from
him if he didn't hurry.
"And I love you."

She stared at him.
Didn't know what to say.
What to do.

But he knew
what he wanted to do.

He leaned in
to kiss her,
his dark eyes
begging her to
let him.

She put her arms out
and stopped him.

"No," she told him.
"We can't."

"Yes, we can."

She shook her head.
"But we won't."

And then she turned,
and walked away.

It was the first
and last time
Vince ever tried
to kiss her.

THE CAR stops and the engine is turned off. Carl opens one eye, just barely.

"We need to get him inside," a woman's voice says. "We have to stop the bleeding."

"Mom, does it really matter? I mean, we're all going to—"

"Yes," she hisses. "It matters. We're all he has, and we're going to do the right thing." She pauses. "I have to believe, that despite the insanity, there are still some people doing the right thing. And we're going to be some of those people, okay?"

"Okay."

Carl tries to sit up. Maybe he can get up and walk so they don't have to drag him inside. But as soon as he tries, he gets dizzy.

His head falls back against the seat, and his eyes close again.

EMERSON SITS on one of the benches at the edge of the mansion's enormous lawn. They overlook the city of Portland, and in daylight, she imagines it is quite the view. Even now, looking down on the city that's lit up in the darkness, it's beautiful.

When she spotted the benches, after walking around for a few minutes, she didn't think it made sense to actually take a seat. After all, it was supposed to be a simple kiss. A kiss doesn't take long.

At least, it shouldn't take long.

But then, Vince and Kat didn't come out. And so Emerson sat down, like she's there specifically to enjoy the view and sitting on the bench at five o'clock in the morning all by herself is completely and totally normal. Of course, it's really not normal. And she's having trouble actually enjoying the view when she can't stop imagining what might be going on in that teensy-tiny bedroom.

As time goes on, she realizes her anxiety is turning to anger. This is not right, him leaving her out here, all alone, in the dark, for this long. It's inconsiderate and rude and just plain wrong. She decides she's going to let him know that when he finally shows his face again.

How will he even have the nerve to show his face again?

Like she won't know what he's been doing? Of course she knows. Will he joke about it? Try to lighten her mood, which has gone from pretty happy to downright miserable since Kat showed up?

Is he going to want to include Kat in the rest of their day? Their very last day? It's been the two of them for so long, it feels strange to expand their circle at this point. No, not a circle. A pair. A tight-knit, all-we-need-is-you-and-me pair.

Just the thought makes Emerson feel slightly queasy. She doesn't want to follow the two of them around like a lost puppy. No, she'd rather be alone than do that.

And then, their laughter rings out across the yard. Emerson turns, but it's dark, and she can't see them yet.

"Where is she?" It's Vince's voice. "Do you see her?"

For a moment, Emerson thinks about trying to hide. It'd serve them right to worry about her, and spend precious time looking for her. But she's here, in the wide open, and there's nowhere to hide. Besides, she can't deny she's curious about what they'll say to her. How much they'll disclose about what happened between them.

So, she stands up. And they appear from the shadows. "There she is," Kat says.

Emerson watches as they walk toward her. They're not holding hands, but Kat kind of leans into him as she walks, like she wishes they were.

"Hey," he says when they reach Emerson. "Sorry. We, uh, got to talking and lost track of time."

"Don't do that," Emerson says through gritted teeth. "Don't insult my intelligence, Mr. Say-One-Thing-and-Do-Another."

"Wait. Are you, like, mad right now?" Kat asks.

"Yes," Vince says, holding Emerson's gaze. "Yes, she is."

Kat holds out her hands as if to say, *What's the big deal?* "But why?"

Vince crosses his arms. "I'd actually like to know the answer to that question, too."

"You guys left me out here while you did who-knows-what in that bed that isn't even yours," Emerson yells. "I mean, gross! And rude."

Vince steps forward, tries to touch her, but she steps back. "Girl, come on. You know it wasn't like that."

"No. I don't. And I can't believe you're standing here, lying about it. Like I'm that stupid."

Vince turns to Kat. "I'm sorry, but maybe it'd be better if you went home for a while."

Kat looks at him, confused. "But I thought you said we could—"

Emerson throws her hands in the air. "You know what? No. I don't want to be alone with you. I just want to be alone, as in by myself. So please, why don't you two leave and go back to whatever it is that you were doing before guilt crept in and you decided you'd better come and find me? I'm just going to sit here and wait for daylight. I bet the view is amazing."

She goes back to the bench and plops down, wrapping her arms tightly around herself.

"Don't you want me to show you your surprise?" Vince asks.

"No."

"Emerson—"

"I said I want to be alone."

Emerson's back is turned to them now, so she can't see what they're doing. She hears some whispering, and then, there's nothing.

It's a long time before she finally takes a peek to see if they're gone. When she discovers they are, she pinches her lips together, and blinks back the tears.

She tells herself it's what she wanted. Though she knows it really wasn't.

BIRDS CHIRP like it's another ordinary day. After all, they don't know any better. Emerson watches as light trickles into the sky. She's facing the east, and because she's above the city, it's the perfect vantage point to watch the sun tiptoe its way into view. Soon, sunlight and clouds swirl together, and it's like the sky is one big Creamsicle.

Deliciously lovely.

For a long time, her life had been ugly. Some days, the ugliness depressed her so much, she wanted to sit and do nothing. But Vince made a game out of looking for beauty in ordinary things in an effort to cheer her up.

"It's everywhere," he told her once. "You'll be amazed all the places you can find it when you keep your mind open to it."

So they would look. And he was right; they found it just about everywhere. In posters advertising the latest exhibit at the art museum. In a dandelion growing in the grass. In the way a tree's leaves fluttered in the breeze. In the eyes of an old woman. In the laughter of a child.

As she remembers the things they discovered, she gasps. Now it all makes sense. When he said it wasn't ready yet, he meant he couldn't show her the surprise because it was too early.

This is it—the sunrise. He brought her here to see it, knowing that from this vantage point, it would be beautiful beyond words.

She's about to get up, to run back to the chauffeur quarters and see if Vince and Kat happen to be hanging out there. Or the parking lot, where they might have sat in the car, giving her some time. Because although they left, her heart tells her Vince wouldn't really leave her. Not completely, anyway.

But as she's about to run and find him, he's there. Sliding in next to her, on the bench.

"Pretty spectacular, right?" he says softly.

He's looking out at the sky, but all Emerson can do is stare at him. She was right—he didn't leave. Or he left, changed his mind, and came back. Whatever. He's here. And she's so relieved, she can hardly breathe.

"Where's Kat?" Emerson whispers.

He looks at her. "She went home."

"Do you like her?"

"Are you jealous?"

"Stop it. I just want to know."

"Emerson, nothing happened. I mean, not like what you think. We talked. We kissed, because we had a deal. Then we talked some more. She's sad. Kind of lonely, you know? Like a lot of people right now." He touches her face, and turns it slightly, toward the sunrise. "Now, stop talking. I don't want you to miss your surprise."

Emerson scoots down to get comfortable, and leans into Vince. He puts his arm around her and she curls up next to him. Together they watch as splendor and light extinguish the darkness completely.

It's hard to watch it and not wish for a hundred more like it. A thousand more. Ten thousand more.

On any given day, this sunrise would be an amazing spectacle. Today, armed with the knowledge of what's coming, it brings tears to her eyes. If she could have one wish, Emerson is sure it would be for time to stop right now, in this moment. But of course, Mother Nature isn't in the wish-making business.

So the sun rises. And the message is sent loud and clear.

Time is ticking.

When the impressive show is over, Emerson turns to Vince. "Yes. I was jealous."

He smiles a really big smile. "I knew it."

"You swear nothing happened?"

He raises his hand. "On my mother's grave."

"While you were busy talking, *Mr. Casanova*, I had a lot of time to sit here and think. And I realized something."

He looks at her curiously. "And?"

She swallows hard. "And, I realized I've been afraid. Afraid because I didn't want more pain in my life. This whole time, I've been playing it safe, like Rima back in the library. But you know what? There are no amazing sunrises back in that library. She's missing out."

He nods. "Truth."

"I don't want to miss out anymore," Emerson says in almost a whisper. "I was telling myself that I don't deserve the good stuff." She sits up straighter. Her voice is louder now. "But it's not true. I deserve it as much as anyone. Certainly as much as that devil disguised as a girl you made out with."

Vince laughs. "Em, come on."

"No, let me finish. Because, you know what else? The crazy thing is, I was afraid I'd get hurt by you." She rolls her eyes. "God, why don't I just get a tattoo across my forehead that says *idiot*?"

"Stop it. You're not an idiot."

"Yes. I am. Because you don't hurt people. Vince, you *help* people. Like, this idiot sitting next to you didn't see what you spell out for me every single day. You are the complete *opposite* of pain." She stretches her arms out. "Like, pain is here." She waves her left hand. "And you are here." She wiggles her right hand.

He gives her half a grin. "And so?"

"So. As I thought about that, I realized, you are my Mr. Darcy."

"Wait. Just a second ago you said I was Mr. Casanova."

She gives his leg a little shove. "I was joking."

"Okay. I'm Mr. Darcy. Is that a good thing?"

Emerson leans forward. "Trust me. A very good thing."

And then, before he can say any more, she puts her lips, gently, on his. It's so tender at first, and silky soft, it takes her breath away. It's only a few seconds before he pulls her to him, their lips parting ever so slightly, and he tastes like fresh air with a hint of peppermint. She starts to pull away and ask if Kat had mints or gum she shared with him, but she resists. After all, now is not the time for an inquisition. Especially about something as ridiculous as why he tastes like mint.

She tells herself to simply enjoy it. All of it. His kisses. His touch. Him. She runs her hands across his big, broad shoulders. One of his hands moves down her spine and comes to rest at the small of her back, where he presses her closer, even though they are about as close as they can be. As her hands float down to his chest, Emerson is sure nothing has ever felt so good and so right as this.

And then, behind her closed eyes, she sees stars. Stars full of light and love. To kiss him is to sail across the night sky. To travel on a moonbeam. To dance across stardust. Where there are stars, there are wishes. A hundred, a thousand, a million, all the same.

*Let us live so we can love.*

Eventually, Vince's mouth leaves hers, and he's breathing hard as he kisses her cheek, her jaw, her neck, and then her ear. She can't help but shiver.

When he whispers, "I love you, Elizabeth Whatever-Your-Last-Name-Is," she bursts out laughing.

She leans back, a smile as wide as the Hawthorne Bridge, and says, "The name's Emerson Steele. And I love you, too, Vince Mason."

THEY SIT
on the bench
wrapped in each
other's arms
kissing
and kissing
and more kissing
still.

They drink
each other up
like a magical potion
that provides
immortality.

If only.

The sun continues
to rise.
It grows warmer,
time passes
and still,
they don't move

from the spot
above the city,
on the hill
near the mansion.

For now,
there is nothing to see.
Nothing to do.
Nothing to miss.

It's like a song that
pulls you in and
fills you up
and gives you what
you didn't even know
you needed until
the sounds, the melody,
and the voices
wash away the pain.

They have each other,
and it's all they need.

A new single,
headed for the top
of the charts.

"Hɪ."

Carl feels someone poking his nose and he opens his eyes. There's a blurry little person with blue eyes and curly blond hair staring at him. But that isn't what concerns him most. He's instantly aware of how much the back of his head hurts. When he reaches back he finds a huge bump.

"Ow," he says with a moan.

"Oh, sweet pea, you need to leave him alone," the woman says, scooping the little girl into her arms. Carl gets a whiff of her stale coffee breath and recoils. "Here," she continues, talking to the girl. "Why don't you watch a movie on the tablet? I've got it all set up. Sit in the chair with Mr. Monkey and put your headphones on."

Once the child is situated, the woman turns back to Carl. "Sorry about that. She was just being friendly."

Carl sits up slowly, wishing his head would stop throbbing. He manages to open one eye slightly.

"Should I get you some more acetaminophen?" the woman asks.

"Yes, please," Carl says.

"I gave you two before," she says. "After you stumbled into the house, with myself and my daughter on either side of you, trying to hold you up. Do you remember?"

"Not really," he says.

"So you want a couple more? Pain pills, I mean."

"How about three? Or maybe even four?"

"You don't want to overdo it," she says.

"At this point," he says, leaning back against the back of the sofa, "I don't think it matters much."

When she steps away, he takes a look around. It was dark earlier and he couldn't see much. It's a nice house. Cozy. Kind of old. He notices a curio cabinet in the corner filled with vases in various sizes and colors. To his right is the kitchen, and he can see the woman moving around in there.

She brings him the pills and a bottle of water. "I wasn't sure if I should let you sleep. After we got you cleaned up, I mean. I think a person is supposed to stay awake after a concussion."

"Like I said," Carl says as he unscrews the cap on the bottle of water, "at this point, I don't think it matters much."

The woman sits down at the far end of the sofa. "I'm sorry that happened to you. It's terrible, the way they knocked you out so they could take your car."

Carl pops the pills into his mouth and drains the water bottle. It hurts to think. To try to remember. His brain is so fuzzy, it's like he's swimming through split-pea soup.

The woman keeps talking. "Thank goodness we found you. We normally wouldn't be in downtown Portland in the middle of the night, of course, but we've been looking for my middle daughter. My oldest daughter, Frankie, is desperate to find her. She's the one who helped me get you in and out of the car. Little Paige was asleep in her car seat. I was exhausted and had told Frankie it was time to come home when we found you."

She's talking so fast. It's too many words, and Carl wants to ask her to slow down. Or maybe stop talking altogether. He starts to ask her if she can please take him home soon. He realizes she's done a lot for him, but surely she'll understand that he wants to go home. No, *needs* to go home. But before he can get the words out, the woman reaches over to the end table and picks up a frame with a picture in it.

"This is my other daughter," she says. "The one we've been looking for. She ran away about a year and a half ago. We checked all the shelters and someone finally told us he recognized her. Apparently, she's been staying at a youth shelter. She wasn't there at the time, but at least we know she hasn't left Portland."

Carl blinks his eyes, trying hard to focus. She moves the picture closer, like she can tell he's having trouble seeing.

"Are you all right?" she asks as he stares at the photo. "You don't look so good. Maybe you better lie back down. Shoot, I just realized I haven't even asked you your name."

"Carl," he tells her, though that's not what he wanted to tell her. There's something about that picture. What is it? He tries to figure out why this girl looks familiar, but his head hurts so much, and there's ringing in his ears, and suddenly he feels . . .

"Oh no," cries the woman as Carl leans forward and vomits all over the pretty beige carpet. She throws the picture down, mutters a couple of curse words, and runs toward the kitchen. "Don't worry. I'll get it cleaned up. Maybe you should lie down. Rest some more."

It's the only thing that makes any sense at the moment. So he returns his head to the nice, soft pillow she brought him last night, closes his eyes, and does as she says.

"I'M SORRY it took me so long," Emerson says, running her finger down Vince's strong jawline.

He kisses the tip of her nose. "You know what they say. Better late than never."

As she tries to draw up her leg and curl it in front of her, a sharp pain shoots down her back. "Ow."

"What?"

She turns, facing forward on the bench, her hands massaging her sides. "My back. I think I need to get up and walk around."

Vince stands up, then leans down and carefully, tenderly, helps Emerson to her feet. "You all right?"

She smiles as she stretches her arms up toward the sky, twisting her body right and then left. "I'm good. Just a little stiff. We, um, sat there a long time."

When she's done stretching, he takes her hand and they walk slowly along the pathway that curves around the viewing area, with the city below. The air smells clean. Fresh. Emerson takes a deep breath and holds it in.

"I'm starving," Vince says.

"Yeah. Me too. Wish we could have a big breakfast. You know—eggs, bacon, hash browns, toast. The works."

"That does sound good."

"What are we doing today, anyway? Do you want to help more people, or . . ."

Her voice trails off. It's their last day. Ever. Suddenly, it seems so final. And so important that they get it right. Whatever they do, it needs to be right. They can't mess up on this. There's no tomorrow. No second chances.

They stop walking and take in the view. Emerson feels her chest tighten as she thinks about all of it, gone, in a matter of hours. How does a person come to terms with it? Like, how do people with terminal diseases do it? Accept it? She's about to ask Vince, when he turns to her and says, "I want to help one more person."

Emerson looks at him, puzzled. "You do? Well, it might be harder to find someone today. I mean, will people be out and about?"

"It won't be hard."

"It won't?"

"No."

"How come?"

He smiles. "Because the person we're going to help is you."

Emerson shakes her head slightly. "I don't get it."

"Do you remember what Carl said? The last thing he said? Before we left the bridge."

She thinks back to their conversation. "Look for those who have wishes or regrets?"

"Exactly. You have both. And you shouldn't. It'll be hard for you, as the day goes on. It'll get harder and harder. More and more painful. And I don't want it to be that way for you. If we go and see your mom and sister today, you can be free of all that, you know?"

"It's sweet, that you're thinking of me. Worrying about me. But I don't know if I'm up to it. I mean, what if it doesn't go the way I hope? Won't I feel worse?"

"The way I see it, it can only go one way. Because it's now or never, baby. This is it. You gotta make things right, and I think everyone is going to want that."

Emerson sighs and turns back to the view. He sounds so sure. And it makes sense. It does. But it's hard to let go of the fear she's been carrying around for so long. After all, her mother made Emerson leave.

"You weren't there, Vince. You didn't see the way she looked at me. The way she screamed and cried, furious at me. I'm just not sure—"

He takes her arm and spins her around so she's facing him. A slight breeze catches her hair, and she has to brush it away from her face. Vince looks so serious. And determined. "She was mad at the time, I get that. But it's not the same world it was then, Em. And besides, time has this magical ability to change things. Just because something was true then doesn't mean it's true today. I know it's hard to believe in magic, but I think it's time for you to try. I never want to hurt you. You know that. I wouldn't do this if I didn't believe that your family will be happy to see you."

He reaches out and takes both of her hands in his, and caresses them with his thumbs. It instantly eases the tension she feels just thinking about doing what he's suggesting.

"I'm scared," she says softly.

"I know. I get it. I do. But I'll be with you the entire time."

"And when it's over, can we go somewhere, the two of us? Somewhere nice? Special?"

He nods and gives her that half grin she loves so much. "Absolutely."

She takes a deep breath. "Okay."

He raises his eyebrows. "Okay?"

"Yeah. Let's do it. After we get something to eat."

He turns and starts walking back, toward the mansion, holding her hand as he goes. "While you're jonesing for a big breakfast, I'm hungry for some mac and cheese."

"Like, from a box?"

He shakes his head. "No way. Homemade, with three kinds of cheeses and bread crumbs on the top. Like my mom used to make."

The way he says it, she feels like someone's reached in and pinched her heart. "I'm sorry, Vince. That you only have me."

He stops walking and looks at her. His face is stern. "Don't be sorry about that. You can be sorry I don't have my mom, but you can only be happy I have you. Because that's what I am—happy as that Schroeder kid in the *Peanuts* gang when he's playing the piano."

Emerson laughs. "He does like his piano, doesn't he?"

"He sure does," Vince says, pulling her into him for a quick kiss. "You remember that, okay? You, girl, are my piano."

"**WHAT ABOUT** you?" she asks when they get into the car.

"What about me?"

"You want to help me. Maybe we should help you, too."

Vince turns the key and puts the car into drive. "I'm not following you. I don't have anyone to make up with. Not like you."

"We could visit your mom's grave. Take her flowers, maybe?"

He glares at her. "That's stupid. I don't need to do that. I made peace with it a long time ago."

She picks at a fingernail, wondering if she should go further. From time to time, she sees glimpses of the feelings he works hard at hiding, and it makes her sad for him. What he's gone through is worse than anything she's experienced. If she needs to deal with things left undone, shouldn't he do the same?

"Are you sure about that?" she asks with trepidation, knowing he's probably not going to take the question well. "About being at peace?"

He stops the car and puts it into park. "What are you doing, Emerson? Because whatever it is, you need to stop. Right now."

"I'm sorry, it's just . . . I don't want you to have any regrets, either. Maybe you'd feel better if you went and visited her one more time. Sometimes I get the feeling that you're—"

"That I'm what?"

She says it quietly, hoping she doesn't upset him. "Pissed off. About her dying and leaving you all alone."

"Well, you're wrong."

"So, you don't want to go see her?"

He grits his teeth, then takes a deep breath. "See her? Emerson, it's not *her*. It's a grave."

"Okay, but it's the only way you can visit her. I mean, you're making me see my family, so—"

"It's not the same!" he yells. "You don't know anything, Emerson. About any of it. Which is why you need to leave it alone."

"That's right," she says, louder now as she glares at him. "I don't know anything because you won't tell me. All I know is your mom died, you lived in some crappy places, and then you ran away. Why won't you tell me more?"

He groans as he squeezes the steering wheel so hard, his arms quiver. "Because, what good would that do? Don't you get it? I don't want to relive any of it. It's gone. Over. There's nothing I can do to change the hand I was dealt. Any chance of something good happening lies ahead of me, not behind me. I've got to keep moving forward, so please, stop trying to pull me back there."

"Then why can't I do that, too?" she asks, her voice softer again. "Why can't I move forward with you, and forget about everything else?"

He shakes his head as he puts the car into drive. "Because,

girl. Your family is here. Alive, you know? And maybe that isn't a big deal to you, but believe me, it is."

Emerson doesn't know what to say.

As Vince turns the corner and heads down the road, he says, "When you hug them, you'll be glad."

"How do you know for sure?"

"Because no one regrets a hug. You only regret not giving one when you had the chance and didn't take it."

*A missed opportunity*

**IT HAD** been raining
for weeks.

Dreary.
Gray.
Hopeless.

It felt like
Mother Nature had
her heart broken
and everyone was forced
to suffer along with her.

It was a Sunday morning
when Kenny came into Emerson's room
and told her to get up.
He needed her to hold
the ladder while
he cleaned out the gutters
of the two-story house.

She'd been out late the night before.
Nothing sounded worse than

getting out of her warm bed
and standing in the pouring rain.

"Get Frankie to do it,"
she muttered.

"No, Emerson," he said.
"We talked about this yesterday.
She helped me clean out the garage.
It's your turn.
Now get up. Let's go."

She refused.
He yelled.
She put the pillow over her head.
He reached down and yanked her up.

She struggled and slapped.
He wrestled and wrangled.

He held her tight as he said,
"Get dressed. Now."

"All right!" she screamed.
"Let me go."

Her mother appeared,
as Emerson staggered across the floor,
to her dresser,
telling herself not to cry,
not to cry,

not to cry,
because she would not give
him that satisfaction.

"What's going on?" her mom asked.

"She wasn't cooperating at first," he said.
"But she is now. Everything's fine, don't worry."

Her mother sighed.
Rubbed her large belly as if
it might grant her three wishes.
"I'm so tired of you two fighting."

Emerson spun around,
rage firing the movement.
"He barged in here and dragged me
out of bed! Who does that?"

"She wouldn't get up," he replied.
"And we've got to get those gutters clean."

"You couldn't wait a few hours?" her mom asked.

"No," is all he said to her.
"Be out there in ten," he yelled at Emerson
before he stormed out.

Once he was gone,
Emerson let the tears fall.
"Mom," she whispered.

One word.
One tiny, little word.
And in it,
a longing,
a wish,
a prayer.

What Emerson wanted
in that moment
was so simple, really.

Why didn't her mother know it?
See it?
Feel it?

They were only a few steps away.
In seconds, she could have been there,
holding her daughter,
consoling her,
telling her everything would be all right.

Instead, she said,
"Hopefully, it won't take too long.
Then you can go back to bed."

As her mom left the room,
Emerson wondered if
it was all she had to give
or all she wanted to give.

She listened to
the rain fall outside.

Gray.
Dreary.
Hopeless.

## 10:02 a.m.

IT IS the headache from hell that won't quit. Carl drifts in and out of sleep. Or maybe consciousness. He's not sure which, and wonders if it matters. All he knows is if he stays very, very still, with his head resting on the nice, soft pillow, and doesn't open his eyes, he can keep the nausea at bay.

He wishes he had his wife by his side to comfort him.

*Soon*, he tells himself.

*Hopefully soon.*

EMERSON DECIDES she needs to say one more thing. "Vince?"

"Yeah?"

"If you think of something you want to do, something for yourself, will you promise to tell me?"

He pulls into a grocery store parking lot, parks the car, and turns to her. "I promise."

She leans in and gives him a quick kiss. "Good. That makes me feel better. Now can we go find some food?"

"Absolutely. That's why we're here."

"I hope there's something left."

They get out of the car and head toward the front doors, which are wide open. Maybe the owners figure if people need food, they'll find a way to get in. Might as well make it easy for people.

"Who knows?" Vince says. "We might get lucky and find some pork rinds and Twinkies."

"Well, I could probably eat a Twinkie, but fried pork rinds?" She shudders. "I think I'd rather starve."

It's not like she hasn't gone hungry before. She's familiar with the gnawing pain in the belly when it's been hours, or even days, since there's been food to eat. They ate well yesterday, so she knows she could get through today just fine. And

Vince could, too, if he wanted to. But right now, with things going so well the past twenty-four hours, it's like he doesn't want to stop. They barely got by for so long, it makes sense that he wants to make the most of their newfound freedom and all the benefits that come with it.

Once they're in the store, they scan the mostly empty shelves for anything that sounds good. There are some cans of soup and lots of beans, but of course they don't have a way to heat them up.

They pass a skinny red-haired woman and a couple of deathly pale guys with greasy hair and dark shadows under their eyes. *Druggies,* Emerson thinks to herself. Vince puts his arm around Emerson's shoulders protectively. When they reach the end of the aisle, she turns around and watches them. "Let's find something and get out of here," she whispers. "They're giving me the creeps."

"Okay."

The next aisle over, they find a lonely box of doughnuts and grab it. Vince also snags the last bag of chips: Fritos.

"Frankie's favorite," Emerson tells him.

"Yeah?"

"She was crazy for them, but Mom had this thing against chips of any kind. I don't know what the deal was, exactly, just that they weren't allowed in our house. Anyway, I caught Frankie eating some in her room one time, and Miss Goody Two-shoes was really freaked out about it. She made me swear I wouldn't tell Mom. I used it to my advantage, of course."

"What'd you get in exchange?"

"She let me wear one of her shirts to a party I was planning to sneak out to that night. And she didn't tell Mom about the sneaking out part, either. One of my better deals, I must say."

As Emerson thinks of her mom and sister, butterflies come rushing back into her stomach at the thought of seeing them again.

It's been so long.

Maybe too long. What if it's too late to try to repair things? Vince is so sure they want to see her, but he doesn't know. He wasn't there when it all went down. What if Mr. Optimistic is wrong about it all?

"Oh," Vince says, stopping right before they get to the front doors, "you know, we should get some water, too. Or something to drink anyway."

Emerson takes off running. "Back in a flash."

Of course, there are no bottles of water or juice to be found. Emerson turns around, deciding she'll try to find the soda aisle on her way out, when she sees what appear to be two young teen girls, hiding in a corner, their knees curled up into their chests and their heads full of strawberry-blond hair resting in their arms. One of them raises her head and stares at Emerson.

She walks over to them. "Hey. Are you okay?"

The other girl looks up, too, tears streaking down her face. As Emerson studies her, she realizes the two girls are identical twins.

"What's it to you?" says the one who isn't crying.

"I don't know," Emerson says, surprised by the girl's anger. "I saw you sitting here, and thought maybe I could help. Do you need a ride or something?"

The other girl pipes in. "Our mom took off with a couple of guys. Just left us here. Said she'd come back for us in a while, but what are we supposed to do until then?"

Vince walks up carrying the Fritos and the box of

doughnuts and kind of looks around, like he's taking in the situation. "What's going on?"

"I think we need to help these girls," Emerson tells him. "Their mom left." She turns back and asks them, "Did she leave with those two creepy guys? The ones who looked all strung out?"

"Yep," the angry one says. "That's our mother. She really knows how to pick 'em."

"Help them how?" Vince asks Emerson.

Emerson looks around the store nervously. "I don't know. Maybe give them a ride home? Their mom said she'd come back for them, but what if she doesn't? I'm not sure we should leave them here. How old are you girls, anyway?"

"Twelve," they say at the same time.

She gives Vince a look that says, *See? They need us.*

He pulls Emerson back a few steps. "But we had it planned out, remember? We're going to see your family. Because it's important. Time is running out, Em."

"Vince, look at them. We can't leave them here like this. If we did, I wouldn't be able to think about anything else."

He narrows his eyes. "This isn't about you trying to get out of something you're scared of doing?"

"I'm not thinking about any of that right now, okay? All I know is I want to help them. I *have* to help them. What's wrong with continuing what we did yesterday?" She folds her hands in front of her. "Please? Besides, it's still early in the day, right?"

He thinks on it for a moment, and then nods. "All right. Let's do it."

They turn back to the girls. "Come on," Emerson says. "Let's get you home. Your mom will know to go there if she doesn't find you here, right?"

"Hard to say," the sad one says as she stands up. "But at least we'll feel safer at home."

"Maybe we can leave a note," Emerson says. She looks at Vince. "Can you run to the car and get a pen from the glove box?"

He doesn't reply, just takes off toward the parking lot.

The girl on her feet helps the angry sister up as she says, "I'm Kailee, by the way, and this is Kendall."

Emerson quickly looks the girls over, trying to determine how she's going to tell the two apart. Kailee's hair is smoother. Shinier. Like she uses product and blows out her hair, while Kendall lets it go natural. Kendall has a lot more curl to her hair. She makes a mental note before she says, "Nice to meet you both. I'm Emerson and my friend is Vince."

He's back in record time, with a pen and a piece of paper. Emerson has the girls introduce themselves to Vince while she writes a note.

We took the twins home.
They're waiting for you there.

Emerson puts the note on the floor, where the girls had been sitting. "I hope she sees it."

"We've done all we can do, I think," Vince says. He looks at the girls. "So where are we headed?"

"Well, we were up here visiting my grandma for the night, but we actually live in Salem."

Vince stares at the twins for a moment and then turns and looks at Emerson. "Did you know this?"

"No, but it shouldn't be a problem?" Emerson says. "It's only an hour away. The tank is almost full, so we're good."

He holds up the stuff he's carrying. "Okay. We've got snack foods and a sweet ride, which is all you really need for a road trip. Let's do this."

Emerson grabs a two-liter bottle of diet RC Cola, one of the only drinks left, as they head toward the door.

"I'm excited," Emerson says to Vince when they get to the car. "I haven't been on a road trip in a long time. Maybe we should just keep going. Go see the Grand Canyon or something. Wouldn't that be fun?"

He shakes his head and smiles. "Girl, at some point, you have to stop running. You get that, right?"

"I was just teasing," Emerson says.

Although she *has* always wanted to see the Grand Canyon.

IT'S QUIET at first, as they head toward the freeway. Vince and Emerson munch on snacks and guzzle down soda.

"You want some?" Emerson asks, glancing behind her, at the girls in the backseat. "Vince and I are firm believers in the *caring-is-sharing* philosophy. Except when it comes to the flu or other communicable diseases, of course."

"Sure," Kailee says. "Grandma was still sleeping when we left, so we didn't get breakfast. Mom didn't want to have to say good-bye."

Emerson passes the food and drink to the back.

"It can be hard, that's for sure," Vince says.

"But she knew you were leaving, right?" Emerson asks.

Kailee is taking a swig of soda, so Kendall answers. "She didn't have a clue. Mom hadn't said how long we were staying. We weren't even sure. We just hoped we could get back and spend today with Teddy."

Emerson looks at them quizzically. "Teddy? Who's that?"

"Our Australian shepherd," Kailee says as she hands Kendall the soda. "You can meet him if you want. He's the sweetest dog you've ever seen."

"But you left him alone?" Emerson asks.

"Yeah, in the backyard," Kailee says. "We wanted to take him with us, but Mom insisted that was the worst idea ever."

"You guys must be thinking she deserves the Mother of the Year award," Kendall says with a hint of disgust in her voice.

Emerson starts to say they're not alone with their mommy issues, but she decides against it. Instead, she leaves it to Vince to say the right thing.

"It's a really strange time right now," he says. "I think some people just don't know how to handle it."

"Well, I can tell you that ditching your daughters for two scumbags is definitely *not* how to handle it," Kendall says. "And anyone with half a brain, or heart, would know that."

It gets quiet then, and the girls each take a doughnut from the box. Emerson turns up the stereo, thinking back to what Mr. Bow-tie said about music's healing powers.

"Mmm, I like this song," Kailee says, bobbing her head to the music.

"Doughnuts and Justin Timberlake," Kendall says happily. "Now *this* is an awesome last day."

"Hey, I've got a question for you guys," Vince says. "If you could go back and relive one day, which day would it be?"

"Like, relive it because it was so awesome?" Kailee asks. "Or relive it so you could do it over because it was completely terrible?"

"Let's go with awesome," Vince says. He looks at Emerson. "You go first."

"You mean, besides this morning?"

He reaches over and strokes her hair, glancing at her briefly. The look in his eyes makes Emerson blush. "Yeah. Besides this morning."

**BEFORE HER** mom
told her to leave.

Before she had to
change schools.

Before her life
turned upside down.

She had friends,
and she had fun.

One summer day in August,
it was the kind of hot
that makes people
flock to malls and
movie theaters to cool off.

Her friend
Annie invited her
to go waterskiing
with her older brother, Chris,
and his best friend, Paul.

As she imagined the day
spent on a cool lake,
with cute boys in a boat,
Emerson thought,
this must be how
Charlie felt when he
found a golden ticket for
the chocolate factory.

And the day
did not disappoint.

The lake was a beautiful
cobalt blue and
bone-chilling cold.

She'd never been
waterskiing before,
and it took her a few times
to get the hang of it.

But once she got up,
she wanted to stay there,
flying across the water,
the warm sun on her face,
the cool spray on her legs.

They took turns,
and when she wasn't skiing,
she was flirting with Paul,
who flirted right back.

The best kind of days
are the ones that make
you feel like you are living
inside a kaleidoscope,
twirling and swirling
with dazzling joy.

It doesn't happen often.
But when it does,
you hold on tight and
wish for the delight to
go on
and on
and on.

Forever.

CARL WONDERS how long he's been on the sofa. It feels like it's been a long time, but he's not sure. He hears muffled voices coming from the kitchen area. Are they talking about him? Trying to figure out how to get him home? Because he told them, didn't he?

He must have told them how desperately he's trying to get home.

Or did he?

It's so hard to remember what's been said. How much the lady who talks too fast knows about his situation.

These are the things he knows:

She found him on the street.

With the help of her daughter, they brought him here, to their house.

His car had been stolen. Except, he didn't have a car. He was going to take someone else's. Someone he'd just met.

It takes him a minute to remember his name, but finally, he does.

Jerry. He was going to take Jerry's car. But someone knocked him out and they took it instead. The lady who lives in this house and her daughter came by and found him. They were looking for her other daughter downtown. Because she's a runaway.

There was something about her picture that seemed hauntingly familiar.

He wants to see it again. To sit up and study it more closely. And to tell them he has to get home very soon.

But he stays still, with his eyes closed. Because anything else right now seems almost impossible.

WHEN EMERSON finishes her story of the waterskiing day, Vince says, "Sounds like a great day. But I don't like that Paul guy."

Emerson smirks. "No? And why's that?"

"How old were you? Like, twelve? Talk about robbing the cradle."

"Thirteen, I think. And honestly, I flirted with him more than he flirted with me. I was probably just a stupid kid to him."

"Were you wearing a bikini?"

Emerson gives him a friendly shove. "All right, that's enough, Mr. Make-a-Mountain-Out-of-a-Molehill."

He gives her a sideways glance. "All right, Granny Steele. Where'd you get that one? Watch a lot of *Little House on the Prairie* when you were younger?"

"No, actually, I got it from Buzz. Remember how we tried to tell him to go to the doctor? That's what he said. Told us we were making a mountain out of a molehill."

One of the girls clears her throat in the back, a gentle reminder that Vince and Emerson aren't alone.

"Anyway," Emerson says. "I told you mine. Now you tell us yours."

Emerson turns and watches Vince's face, wondering if she'll see any signs of regret for coming up with this game or

159

whatever it is. After all, it's going to force him to talk about something from his past, when he was pretty adamant a little while ago that it's the last thing he wants to do.

But he doesn't flinch. "Man, it's hard to pick one," Vince says. "I mean, you know I'd take any day my mom and I were together. But I guess, since we're heading down to Salem, there's one day that stands out in my mind. It was a summer day, too, though not as hot as your day, Em. I think it was Labor Day, the day before school starts. I can remember the warm temperature with the cool breeze as we made our way around the fairgrounds. It was the Oregon State Fair, and to my little self at the time, it seemed like a pretty wonderful place. The smell of curly fries and corn dogs floating through the air. The way my stomach felt after we rode on the roller coaster. How it seemed like we were on top of the world when we stopped at the highest point on the Ferris wheel."

"How old were you?" Emerson asks.

"I don't know, six or seven probably. I wanted to go on some of the bigger rides, but Mom wouldn't let me. Said they'd make me sick." He smiles. "But we went on the carousel *three* times in a row." He glances at Emerson before he turns his attention back to the road. "Isn't that crazy? She loved that thing. And as I went round and round on my silly painted horse, the cheerful organ music blaring in my ears, all I could think about was how much I wanted to go on the Kamikaze and the Tilt-A-Whirl."

"You probably would have been too short anyway," Kendall says.

Vince chuckles. "Yeah, you're probably right."

"I wonder why she liked it so much," Emerson ponders. "Must have been something special about it, you know?

Maybe it brought back happy memories from her own childhood."

"You might be right. I wish now I'd asked her." He pauses for a moment before he continues. "Anyway, we stayed at the fair all day long. Saw the cows and the big fat mama pig with her litter of piglets. Watched a horse show in the arena. Ate a corn dog."

"What about curly fries?" Emerson asks.

"Those, too. And that's not all. We went to a food booth in the shape of a red barn because my mom said they made the best strawberry shake she'd ever had. And she wasn't kidding. They blended it right there, with fresh milk, ice cream, and real strawberries. I'm telling you, it was like drinking heaven from a straw."

"Okay, now I want a corn dog and strawberry shake," Kendall says.

"Me too," Kailee says.

The car is quiet for a moment. Emerson closes her eyes and tries to remember what a homemade milk shake tastes like, because it's been so long. She made them at home, once in a while, with her mom helping out. They used to make cookies together, too, when she was young. Oatmeal, with chocolate chips. They used the blender and ground up the oatmeal really fine, so they were chewy, but not too chewy.

When Kailee speaks, Emerson's eyes snap open. "Your mom sounds cool. Are you going to see her? After you drop us off?"

Emerson squeezes the door handle, bracing herself, nervous about how he'll respond to her question. But he answers very matter-of-factly. "No. She died when I was eight."

"Oh my gosh," Kailee says, sounding horrified. "Vince, I'm so sorry."

"Hey, it's all right," he says as he glances in the rearview. "You didn't know. And I'm the fool who came up with the silly game, right? Now let's hear yours."

Kendall and Kailee squabble about who goes first, and Emerson tunes them out as she stares at the empty fields they pass along the interstate.

Why is it that people think remembering something good will make them happy? Because a lot of times, remembering something good just makes you sad you're not back there, instead of here.

THEY MAKE it to Salem in record time. The car's navigation system isn't working, so the girls do their best to get them to their house from memory. Before now, they haven't really paid attention to street names, but the twins are good at recognizing landmarks. They make a few wrong turns, but eventually Vince pulls into the driveway of their tiny, rundown house.

"Home, sweet home," Emerson says, turning around and looking at the girls. But they don't seem very thrilled. "What's wrong?"

"I don't know. I kind of feel bad, I guess," Kailee says, looking like she might cry again. "Maybe we should have waited for her."

"No," Kendall says firmly. "We did the right thing. Mom's a big girl. She can take care of herself."

Vince nods. "I think she's right. Now come on, let's go say hello to Teddy."

There's a key under the mat, and Emerson can't help but think about how unsafe that practice is nowadays. Though this place probably isn't high on any criminal's list. The light blue paint is peeling off the siding and the front yard is overgrown, with more weeds than lawn.

"Sorry about the mess," Kendall says as she pushes on

the front door. "We didn't clean up before we took off for Grandma's."

When Emerson steps inside, she can see exactly what Kendall means. There are piles of laundry on the sofa and love seat. Dirty dishes and various food packages cover the coffee and end tables.

They make their way through the family room to the small dining area, where there's a sliding glass door leading to the backyard.

Teddy must have heard the car doors slam or something, because the Australian Shepherd is on his hind legs, scratching at the door, wanting to be let in. The girls rush to see him, opening the door and then dropping down on either side of him. He's gray and black with light brown spots here and there, and a fluffy white chest.

After he lets the twins know how happy he is to see them, he comes over to say hello to Vince and Emerson.

"Oh, Vince, look at his eyes," Emerson says. "One's blue and the other one's brown. Isn't that cool?"

They pet him for a minute, until Teddy turns around and goes back to Kailee and Kendall, who lavish him with more affection.

Vince nervously puts his hands in his pockets as he says, "Well, I guess we should get going. Unless there's anything else you need?"

"Um, can I talk to you for a second?" Emerson asks. She tips her head slightly toward the kitchen nearby. "Alone?"

The girls continue their lovefest with the dog as Emerson and Vince step away. If the family room is a mess, the kitchen is a disaster. Emerson wrinkles her nose at the smell of something bad. Something . . . rotten.

"I don't think we should leave them here alone," she whispers.

Vince scowls. "Why not? This is where they belong. This is where they wanted to come, right? And they're a hell of a lot safer here than that store where we found them."

"I know, but—"

"But what?"

"I feel bad for them," she says as she glances at the counter covered with food-encrusted dishes, pots, and pans. "Can't we do something special for them before we go?"

Vince checks the clock on the microwave, before he answers. "Em. We had a plan. And I love that you're so worried about them and want to help them, but I want to help you. I know I keep saying this, but we don't have a lot of time."

"It's not even noon yet," she replies. "We have time to do a little something fun with them. I mean, come on, isn't it just so depressing, thinking of them sitting in this disgusting place by themselves for the next ten hours or whatever?"

"What do you want to do, exactly?"

Emerson crosses her arms and looks out the small window above the kitchen sink. Her eyes land on a little garden gnome in the flower bed. It makes Emerson smile. He's cute. Friendly looking.

"Maybe we could all go to a park," she says, continuing to stare at the gnome. There's a memory in the far corner of her brain she can't quite reach. She scrunches her forehead trying to grab on to it. It seems like it's important right now.

And then, like the last number on a combination lock, it clicks into place.

She remembers.

BENEATH THE tall trees,
among the delicate ferns,
are bright, colorful flowers,
like something from
a giant Playmobil set.

They aren't real,
those flowers,
which makes them
adorable and silly
all at the same time.

Beside those fake but
fanciful flowers is Alice,
in her blue-and-white dress,
looking up at a caterpillar
sitting on an oversized
mushroom.

And so it goes,
throughout the Enchanted Forest.
Imaginary characters,
from books and fairy tales.

Little Red Riding Hood.
Goldilocks and the Three Bears.
Snow White and the Seven Dwarfs.

It's exactly
what they need.

To step inside
a land of make-believe
when reality
is at its worst.

CARL HAS another dream. This time, he dreams of his wife, sitting on the floor in an empty house, crying.

She cries and cries until he shakes himself awake because he can't take it anymore.

He sits up and yells, "I have to get home."

The woman appears, wringing her hands and looking quite anxious. "Oh, Carl, I don't know if that's a very good idea. You're not well."

"It doesn't matter," he says, not looking up at her. He keeps his eyes focused on the empty glass that sits on the coffee table. He wills himself to sit there, strong and steady.

"Do you have someone at home, waiting for you?" the woman asks.

"Yes. My wife. Her name is Trinity. She's been waiting for me for a very long time, and I just really need to get to her."

"I'm sorry, but I can't take you right now."

Now he looks up at her. "Why not?"

"Because Frankie went to see her dad. We only have the one car."

He sinks back into the sofa cushions. "Will she be gone long?"

"A couple of hours, I'm guessing. Paige begged me to let her go, too." She sighs. "I hope that wasn't a mistake. Paige isn't his kid, so he may not be too happy about the third wheel. Just figured the peace and quiet would be good for you."

He closes his eyes and pinches his nose, because, God, his head hurts.

"Do you need some more pain reliever?" the woman asks him.

He gives her a simple nod, keeping his eyes closed. A minute later, she says, "Here you go. Drink slowly this time. See if you can keep it down."

His eyes flutter open, and she hands him the glass of water and the pills. After he takes them, he hands the glass back to her. "Do you think you could call Frankie? Tell her I need to get home?"

"I can't. The phones are out."

He closes his eyes again. "It feels like I've been trying to get home forever."

The lady sits down next to him. "You sound like Dorothy."

He doesn't respond, because he's not sure what she means.

"You know," she continues. "Dorothy, in *The Wizard of Oz*. Maybe you should try clicking your heels together." He turns his head slightly and looks at her. "Sorry. Probably shouldn't joke about it."

"It's all right," he says. "You're trying to lighten the mood. By the way, I don't know your name, and I feel like if I'm going to continue to camp out on your comfy sofa indefinitely, I should at least know that."

"It's Rhonda."

He takes a deep breath. "Great. Thank you, Rhonda. For everything you've done."

"You're welcome."

"I'm sorry, too," he says. "That you weren't able to find your daughter."

"To be honest, I really didn't expect we'd find her. But Frankie, she just won't give up."

"I have to tell you, when I saw the photo, there's something familiar about her. My brain is just so fuzzy—"

Rhonda sits up straight, her eyes big and round. "Wait. Carl, are you saying you think you've seen her?"

"Maybe," he says. "Actually, yes, I think I have. It's like watching a movie or a television show when I *know* I've seen one of the actors before, but I can't place where."

Rhonda reaches over and gets the framed photo from the end table, and sets it on the coffee table in front of them. They're quiet as they both stare at the girl.

"She's lovely," Carl says.

"She hates me," Rhonda says.

"No. I bet that's not true."

"We had a terrible falling-out," Rhonda explains. "I didn't handle things well. If only I'd known then what I know now."

"I'm guessing a lot of people are saying that today."

"You think so?" Rhonda asks.

"Of course. Pretty sure it'd be impossible today to find anyone who doesn't have at least one regret."

As soon as the last word is out, something snaps in his brain. Literally, it's like a rubber band has been released, and where it was tight and uncomfortable before, it is now loose and relaxed.

Because he knows. He knows where he's seen the girl.

VINCE PULLS into the mostly empty parking lot and parks the car. He and Emerson turn around at the same time, and Emerson grins at the sight of Teddy, sitting in between Kailee and Kendall in the backseat, his tongue hanging out of his mouth. The way his mouth is open and drawn back, it looks like he's smiling. And maybe he is. He gets to go where no dogs have gone before.

"I'm so excited," Kailee says. "We haven't been here in forever."

"It's been a long time for me, too," Emerson says.

"I didn't even know this place was here," Vince says as he opens his door. "The way you described it to me, it sounds like a tiny version of Disneyland."

When they get out of the car, they look up and take in the whimsical buildings, nestled in front of the lush green forest. "I wouldn't go that far," Emerson says. "But it's cute, in its own charming way. You'll see."

They make their way up to the entrance, Teddy pulling ahead of all of them, on his retractable leash. Emerson finds herself feeling a little envious of the dog's happiness. Pure bliss.

After all, he doesn't know what's coming later.

Emerson and Vince walk hand in hand behind the girls, along the trail that takes them to the first "attraction." It's cool under the shade of the tall trees. It feels nice.

Emerson takes a deep breath, filling her lungs with the fresh scent of pine and cedar. "You're not mad, are you?" she asks Vince.

"Not mad. A little disappointed, maybe. I want to make sure there's nothing left undone as far as your family goes, that's all."

She squeezes his hand. "I know. You're a good man, Charlie Brown."

He runs his hand down the Charlie Brown shirt and smiles. They come to Storybook Castle, complete with a small bridge that takes you over a moat filled with water and pastel-colored turrets up high. They step onto the bridge and through the door, where a colorful toy soldier painted on the wall greets them.

They turn the corner as one of the girls up ahead says, "Oh, look. Let's go down to the dungeon!"

As they run ahead, Vince stops and turns to face Emerson. "I don't know. What do you think? You scared of the dungeon?"

"Are you kidding? Dude, that dungeon is posh compared to how we've been living."

He takes Emerson's head in his hands, leans down, and kisses her. Softly. Slowly. When he pulls away, he asks, "It wasn't *that* bad, was it?"

"Easy to say that now," she says, smiling. "Now that we have a BMW, more cash than we need, and an amusement park all to ourselves. Yes, Vince, it was pretty bad."

He takes her hand again and they walk toward the staircase, where the words YE OLDE DUNGEON are written on the wall, along with an arrow pointing down.

"I guess I didn't care that much," he says, stopping again. "I mean, I was with you. Most of the time, that's all that mattered."

"What do you mean, most of the time?"

"Well, you know. There were those days when all I wanted was a big old cheeseburger, and nothing in the world could make that better."

Her stomach rumbles at the thought. "Great. Thanks a lot. Now all I'm going to be able to think about is how much I want a cheeseburger."

Vince narrows his eyes and moves in close. Then he pushes her up against the wall, pressing his body close to hers. He kisses her like they've been apart for a hundred years. Like time and distance and everything else have disappeared, and all that remains is the two of them. They stay wrapped around each other for a couple of minutes, until they hear footsteps coming up the stairs.

When he moves away, eyeing the staircase, Emerson stays standing against the wall, her legs like rubber. She takes a moment to catch her breath before she says, "Well, I guess that's one way to get me to forget about cheeseburgers."

THE FOUR of them giggle their way through Storybook Lane. There's Humpty Dumpty and Little Miss Muffet. There's the Little Old Woman Who Lived in a Shoe with a giant slide they go down again and again. There's Goldilocks and the Three Bears, and the mine where the Seven Dwarfs go to work every day (presumably singing "hi ho, hi ho").

It's a wonderful afternoon for the six-year-olds inside each of them.

When they take a seat at a picnic table after they've seen everything there is to see, they can't help but notice a family sitting at a table a few spots over.

There's a mom, a dad, a little boy, and a little girl. The little girl says something and they all laugh like it's the funniest thing ever. The mom reaches over and wipes the boy's nose with a Kleenex.

It is that small act of tenderness, of concern, of love that hits Emerson like an arrow to the heart. And she's not the only one.

"I think we should go," Kailee says. "We've been gone a while, and if Mom comes home, she'll worry when we're not there."

"*If* she comes home," Kendall says, picking at a piece of chipped paint on the table.

"She's gonna come home," Kailee says. "She has to."

"No, actually, she doesn't," Kendall says.

The back-and-forth is familiar to Emerson. One voice inside her head saying it like it is. The other voice telling it the way she wished it would be. It's reality versus fantasy, and even though you know which one will probably win, you can't help but root for the underdog.

Just once, you want the fantasy to come true.

Just once.

Up until the day her mom told her she needed to go live with her dad, the voices took turns speaking loudly.

Voice #1: Your mom will eventually see Kenny for the man he really is. Just hang in there. She'll kick him out. One day, you'll come home from school, and he'll be gone, and life can go back to normal again.

Voice #2: She loves him more than she loves you. He'll always win, no matter what. Always.

The day her life changed forever, her mom had to choose. Kenny *made* her choose. They'd been waiting up for Emerson, "Worried sick," her mom had said, after she'd discovered Emerson wasn't in her bed. When she got home around three a.m., Kenny laid into her. He told her that her life would be nothing but misery until they could trust her again. No cell phone. No computer. No television. She'd take over all the chores and the cooking so her mom could focus on the new baby.

Emerson couldn't stand that he was the one to bring down the punishment. They weren't related. Hell, he wasn't even married to her mother. As far as she was concerned, he had no right. "You can't make me do any of that. If it makes you feel better to believe that you can, then fine. But you can't. And I won't."

He was furious. Emerson thought he might pop the big blood vessel in the middle of his forehead that stuck out when he got mad. He yelled and screamed, and that made her mom yell and scream. She'd had the baby in her arms, and of course the baby started wailing.

"I can't take this," Kenny yelled when he'd had enough. "It's me or her, Rhonda. This girl is out of control and I refuse to live here with someone who has such disrespect for me. And for you, too. It's not right."

Her mom tried to sweet-talk him then. She talked to him softly, told him it was all a big misunderstanding, and tried to get him to change his mind. When that didn't work, she pulled Emerson into the laundry room and told her she'd better go out there and apologize if she knew what was good for her. Tears streaked down her mother's face as she tried to convince Emerson to "do the right thing."

Emerson held her ground. "I'm not apologizing to him. The way he treats me, he should be the one to apologize. He's not my dad, and he has no right to act like he is." She should have stopped there. She didn't take the time to consider what it might do to her mother. It came out almost like a growl. "I hate him."

And that's when her mom snapped. "You know what, Emerson? I can't deal with your crap anymore, either. It's too much, on top of the baby. I think you need to go and live with your dad for a while. Maybe he'll be able to control you better than we can."

"What? Are you serious?"

"Absolutely. You act like everything should revolve around you, and I'm tired of it. That is *not* how the world works. I'll call your father and tell him to pick you up at four o'clock today. That gives you most of the day to pack."

Two voices, and one of them had been right.

For her, the fantasy hadn't come true. But oh, how she wants it to come true for these girls and their mom.

Kailee ignores her sister's less-than-optimistic comment and looks at Vince. "Would you mind taking us home now, please?"

"You bet," he replies, standing up and digging the car keys out of his pocket. "We should be heading back to Portland anyway."

"It was fun," Kailee says. "Really fun."

"If only today's story ended happily ever after for us," Kendall says as she gets to her feet. Everyone else gets up, too. She looks back at the forest. "I hate thinking about what comes next."

"Then don't think about it," Vince says as they walk down the trail toward the exit. "Stay focused on the right now. Besides, like I was telling Emerson earlier, there's so much more to a story than just the ending. We still have, what, eight hours left or so? That's a ton of time."

The girls look at him like he's crazy.

"Not really a *ton*, Mr. Look-on-the-Bright-Side," Emerson says. She turns to the girls. "He's trying to make us feel better, that's all."

"No, see, you guys are looking at it all wrong," Vince says. "The amount of time isn't important. A hundred minutes or a hundred years. Whatever, it doesn't matter. Just make it count."

"If only it were that easy," Kendall says as she kicks a rock from the pathway.

"Yeah," Kailee says. "It's hard not to be mad that we don't get the hundred years."

Vince shrugs. "Well, maybe you need to ask yourself if that's how you want to spend the rest of your life."

The girls are quiet after that. They reach the car, Vince unlocks it, and everyone climbs in. Emerson turns around, and there's Teddy, wedged between the two girls, with his tongue out as he smiles again.

Vince glances in the rearview and then nods. "See? Teddy's got the right attitude. We all need to be like Teddy."

The girls exchange a look. And then, like they can read each other's minds, they stick their tongues out while trying to smile at the same time.

It is hilarious, and everyone cracks up.

"That's what I'm talking about," Vince says as they pull onto the freeway.

Emerson wants to tell him if he'd like to keep her laughing, the last place she should go is home. But she's guessing Vince would tell her making it count doesn't mean it's always easy and fun.

## EVERY WEDNESDAY
Vince had a ritual.

He went around
and checked on people.

People just like him,
out on the street,
doing their best
to survive.

"How you doing?"
"You need anything?"
"Anyone bothering you?"

Whatever it was
that might be a problem
for someone, he asked.

Maybe he couldn't do
much about it,
but he showed them
that he cared.

He listened.
And he hugged.
A lot.

"Why do you do it?"
Emerson asked him once.

"Because it's terrible
to feel like you've
been forgotten.
To feel like you don't
matter to anyone."

So he helped them
to feel seen and heard.

He wanted them
to know that things
might be difficult
but that didn't mean
no one cared.

Some people think
if you can't give a lot
then what's the point?

But maybe it's like chocolate.

A little bit is better
than nothing at all.

2:15 p.m.

CARL HAS done his best to answer all of Rhonda's questions. He only saw her daughter Emerson for a minute or two, but Rhonda wants to know everything.

"Did she look healthy?"

"Yes."

"Not too skinny, then?"

"No. She looked average, I'd say."

"What was she wearing?"

"Shorts and a T-shirt."

"Was her hair long or short?"

"Long."

"Did she look miserable or happy?"

"Fairly happy."

"Who was she with?"

"A guy, about her age. Maybe older. I don't know."

"What was he like?"

"He had on a Charlie Brown T-shirt. He was nice. Nothing concerning about him at all."

"Did they look like they're in love?"

"Uh . . . I have no idea. How do you tell?"

It was exhausting, but she had done so much for him. He knew he needed to tell her everything he could to put her mind at ease.

Now, after they've shared some leftover chicken noodle soup, they're waiting for Frankie to come back. Carl can't help but wonder why she let Frankie go in the first place. Why couldn't her dad come here instead?

Maybe Rhonda just didn't think it through all the way. It happens. Decisions have to be made, sometimes with very little time, and so, you decide. It's one of the downfalls of being an adult: so many decisions to make.

As the minutes continue to pass, Rhonda paces in front of the sofa. She hasn't said anything in a while. Carl searches the room for a clock, and when he finally spots it, he's surprised by how late it is. All this time, wasted. So many things he'd rather be doing than sitting here, feeling awful, and waiting.

Rhonda stops pacing and looks at Carl. "You said you saw them on a bridge. But you didn't tell me why you were there. Which bridge?"

He swallows hard. "Vista."

She narrows her eyes. "What were you doing up there?"

"It's a long story," he says. "And I'd rather not go into it, if it's all right with you."

"What were they doing up there? Emerson and her friend? Do you know?"

"I don't," he tells her. "But like I told you before, I gave them my wallet when the kid said that's what he wanted most. To have some spending money. Then they turned around and left."

"Are you sure?" she asks. "That they really left, I mean?"

"As far as I know." He rubs his face with his hands. "Shouldn't your daughter be back by now? I really need to get home."

She glances at the clock. "I know. I'm not sure what's taking so long. Maybe she's having a hard time saying good-bye. It can't be easy, right?"

"Oh. Right."

"She'll be here soon," she says. "I could put in a movie if you want. That would kill some time."

The phrase makes him shudder. Who came up with that idiotic saying? Right now that's the last thing he wants to do. Stop time, yes. Savor it, of course. But kill it? No. No way.

Suddenly, he longs to be outside. To feel the sun on his face. To see the sky. The clouds. The trees. Everything.

Anything.

He slowly gets to his feet, for the first time since arriving at Rhonda's.

"Actually, I'd like to see your backyard, if you don't mind," Carl tells her.

"Are you sure you're feeling up to it?"

His head still hurts, but he doesn't tell her that. After he stands there for a moment and is fairly certain he's not going to topple over, he says, "Yes, I'm positive."

She points to the back door. "Go ahead and take a seat on the deck. I'll get us something to drink. Something cold. Refreshing. Yes, that's what we need. No more coffee. I've had way too much today."

He walks toward the door and then stops. "You don't happen to have any cookies, do you? I could really go for some cookies right now."

"All I have are Nilla Wafers. Paige loves them. Would you like some?"

How long has it been since he's had the little, round,

buttery cookies? He thinks it must be decades. And now that she's mentioned them, nothing sounds better.

"Yes, please. I'd love some."

Outside it's warm. Pleasant. He takes a seat in a patio chair, which is surprisingly comfortable. He looks around at the backyard. It's nothing special—just a lawn, a few rhododendron and azalea bushes, and a couple of trees.

But then he sees them. Apples. Small green apples, hanging on one of the trees, and quite a few lying on the ground as well.

He gets up and goes to the tree. He searches until he finds an apple on the ground that isn't too badly bruised, and picks it up. When he takes a bite, it's the kind of tart that makes your lips pucker just a little bit and your heart sigh with joy.

While he takes another bite, he stands there, looking at the tree, thinking about how much he's taken for granted. How many apples has he eaten in a rush, with no regard to the delight of it all?

Too many times.

He takes another bite, but this time, all he can taste is regret.

When Rhonda comes outside, she says, "Oh, good, you've found the apples."

Yes. He wishes he could take them home. Have another apple tomorrow. And the next day. And the day after that. Maybe bake a pie out of them, to enjoy with some vanilla ice cream.

He's found the apples. But it just doesn't seem fair that, soon, he has to let them go.

WHEN THEY turn the corner, onto Thirty-Third Avenue where the twins live, Emerson looks for a car in the driveway.

But there isn't one.

Her heart sinks. "Oh no. I think we made a mistake."

"What do you mean?" Vince asks as he parks along the curb.

"I mean, maybe we should have stayed with them at the store. Waited for her to come back. What if she's looking all over Portland for them? She might not have seen the note. Someone could have taken it, you know? God, I swear, I'm dumber than a rock sometimes."

"Em, you are not. Maybe a little hardheaded once in a while, but that's the only way you are similar to a rock."

"Thanks," she says, lacing it with a bit of sarcasm. "Thanks a lot."

"Look," he says, "we could sit here and do 'what ifs' all day long. Doesn't do us any good right now."

"Personally, I'm glad we didn't stay there," Kendall says. "It wasn't a good place for us."

Kailee doesn't say anything. She just stares out the window, at the empty driveway. Emerson looks at Vince, feeling completely helpless.

"Kailee?" Vince asks as he turns around. "You all right?"

"I can't believe she's not here," she says softly. "I thought . . ." She turns to Kendall. "She should be here."

"But she's not, so you guys have to figure out how you're going to make the most of it," Vince says matter-of-factly. Emerson wonders if that sounds harsh to them. "You've got each other, right? And you've got Teddy." He reaches out and pets Teddy's head. "You've got more than a lot of people have, I promise you that."

"We'll be all right," Kendall says. Emerson can tell she's trying her best to reassure her sister. "Maybe we can bake something delicious."

Kailee perks up a little bit at that idea. "Hey, yeah. We could totally do that. I know we have flour and sugar, and a few eggs left. I'm pretty hungry, actually."

Emerson almost suggests they all go find something to eat, but she knows Vince is anxious to head back to Portland.

"How about if we make cupcakes?" Kendall asks. "We have Grandma's recipe. You know, the chocolate ones she always makes? Pretty sure we have powdered sugar for the icing, too."

"Now you're talking," Vince says. "If we didn't have to get back, we'd stay and help you out with those."

"He means he'd help you eat them, not make them," Emerson teases.

"Hey, I bet I could bake up some fine cupcakes if I got the chance," he says. "I know my way around a kitchen. I made a mean grilled cheese sandwich, once upon a time."

"Okay, we seriously need to stop talking about food before I make like a lion and eat all of you," Emerson says.

"We should go," Kailee says, nudging her sister.

"Thanks so much," Kendall says, looking at Vince and Emerson. "For everything."

"Yeah," Kailee agrees. "Thank you. We're so lucky you offered to help us in the store."

Kendall nods. "Really lucky."

"Well, you girls take care of yourselves," Vince says. "And Teddy, too, of course."

"We will," Kailee says as she opens the door.

"'Bye, you guys," Emerson says. "Thanks for being awesome."

"'Bye," the girls say softly as they get out of the car with Teddy.

Vince and Emerson sit there and watch the girls walk up the driveway toward the front door.

They don't notice the car coming down the street until it turns into the driveway. Kendall and Kailee are at the door, in the process of opening it, when they hear the engine. They turn around and stare, as if they can't quite believe it.

And then, the skinny red-haired woman is getting out of the car and running toward them. If the girls have mixed feelings about seeing her, they don't show it. They simply run toward her, and fall into her arms.

It is a wonderful, happy scene, though Emerson knows that behind the smiling faces, there's a lot more going on. She hopes, for everyone's sake, they can figure out a way to focus on the good stuff.

Vince looks over at Emerson and smiles as he puts the car into drive. "See how easy it is? Just like that."

"I doubt it will be anything like that," Emerson says as they pull away from the house. The girls don't even notice them leave, which, Emerson thinks to herself, is exactly how it should be. "I'm happy for them, though. Maybe she'll help them clean up the kitchen so they can make those chocolate cupcakes."

"And now we can go to Portland guilt-free, right?" Vince says.

"Actually, can we make one quick stop first?" Emerson asks. "I promise it won't take long."

"Where do you want to go?"

She bites her lip as she tries to decide how to respond before she says, "It's a surprise. Just go out to the main street here and head toward downtown Salem."

"Emerson. Really? After our discussion about surprises? Come on. Please tell me."

"No. I'm not going to tell you. Because you might say no. And I really want to do this. So you have to trust me and drive. I'm not sure exactly how to get there, but I'm hoping there will be signs."

He sighs. "Sometimes you're impossible, do you know that?"

She smiles. "Yeah. I've been told that once or twice."

He reaches over and squeezes her shoulder. "But it's part of what makes you . . . you, so I can't really complain, can I?"

"Nope. No complaining." She points her finger straight ahead. "Just driving."

THE SIGN at the top of the building gives it away. SALEM'S RIVERFRONT CAROUSEL.

Vince doesn't say a word as he parks the car by the curb. There doesn't seem to be anyone else here, although the glass windows that used to cover the front of the building are all broken.

"I hope they didn't vandalize it," Emerson says. "That would be horrible."

They step through the shards of broken glass and Emerson pulls on one of the doors, which swings open easily.

The old carousel stands there, as magnificent as ever.

There's graffiti on the walls, and the gift store nearby has been looted. But thankfully, whoever did it left the carousel alone.

"Which horse do you like?" Emerson asks as they walk around and eye the different animals. "Or maybe you want to ride the zebra?"

He stops next to a horse that has a silver shield on its shoulder, and is painted as if it's wearing gold armor, like it's ready for battle. The headdress it wears is teal and gold and beautiful.

Vince gets on the horse.

"I'm going to try and find the on-off switch," Emerson says.

"Look inside that little podium," Vince says, pointing near the place where a person usually stands and takes the tickets.

She steps over to it and sure enough, there's a red button and a green button hidden inside. She presses the green button and a bell rings before the carousel starts to move.

The childlike music plays as the horses move up and down, around and around. Emerson wonders if she should try to jump onto the carousel while it's moving, but decides against it. This is for Vince, after all.

She waves when he comes around and he waves back. Again and again he passes by her, and it's easy to imagine him as an adorable little boy with a big grin on his face, riding the carousel next to his mom.

After a few minutes, Emerson goes back to the pedestal and hits the red button. The carousel slows down. She walks over and waits for it to stop completely.

"How was it?" she asks him.

He hops off his horse. "Honestly? A little lonely."

She steps onto the carousel, walks over, and hugs him. For a long time.

When they separate she says, "I wanted to try and give you a little piece of her, and I thought of coming here after you shared your do-over day with us."

"It was a sweet gesture. Thank you."

"You're welcome."

"It's probably hard for you to understand, but I actually carry a piece of her with me always." He puts his hand over his heart. "Right here."

"But it's not enough, is it? Don't you want more? Aren't you mad you don't get more?"

He turns and stares at the carousel. "Maybe sometimes I am, but I really try not to be. I mean, it's wasted energy, wishing for more. I'd rather spend my time making wishes that might come true."

She laces her fingers through his and leans her head on his arm.

He squeezes her hand as he says, "I'm sorry I yelled earlier. But I really don't want to visit her grave. I know some people like doing that, but I don't." He pauses. "What I have, it's enough."

She turns her face toward him and he kisses her forehead. "Because it has to be?" she asks.

He stares at the carousel again. "Because it has to be."

AS THEY drive back toward Portland, Emerson realizes how tired she feels. Hungry, too. They've been going hard for a lot of hours, and suddenly, all she wants to do is take a moment and rest. Breathe. But Vince is driving fast, like he's on a mission and nothing's going to stop him.

"What's my mom doing right now?" Emerson asks softly as they speed along the freeway.

"Well, she has a feeling you're gonna show up today. A strong feeling. So she's in the bathroom, putting on a little makeup. Wants to look nice for you. She's excited you're coming. And, since I know you're going to ask about your sister next, I'll tell you that she's there, too. She's in the kitchen, baking a cake. They want to be ready to celebrate your homecoming."

Emerson doesn't say anything. She's trying to picture them. Wonders what they look like—how much they've changed since the last time she saw them.

She pictures her mom, run-down. Exhausted. And terribly unhappy, it seemed, in those last days and weeks.

"Vince, please don't be upset with me, but I really don't want to go. I'm tired and hungry and—"

"I know you don't want to go. But you need to."

"Why? If I don't care about seeing them, why do you care so much?"

He slams his hand down, hard, on the steering wheel. "Because, dammit, I would give anything to see my mom today." He turns and looks at her, his eyes cold and hard. "Anything."

"Right. You know why?" She's yelling now, too. "Because your mom was *nice* to you. She loved you more than anything. The way you've opened up and talked about her today, I can tell how much you meant to each other. She never would have kicked you out of her house. But that's what my mother did, and I don't think—"

"You don't get it, do you?"

"Get what?"

"Time is running out!"

"I know that! Don't you think I know that? It's exactly why I don't want to go there." She reaches over and grabs on to his arm. "It could be a huge waste of time, if they don't want to see me."

"Girl, when are you going to stop saying that? Thinking that? Of course they want to see you. And in your final moments, I don't want you to have any regrets. You know why? Regret hurts. Trust me, I know. I think about the last time I saw my mother and all the things I didn't say that I wish I had and . . ." He looks over at her. "It hurts a lot, and it will haunt you forever."

She stares at the digital clock, taking in his words. Her eyes are so heavy. When the clock changes, showing another minute has passed, it makes her jump a little.

"They're family," Vince says, gripping the steering wheel

tightly. "*Your* family. All anyone wants today is to be with their loved ones."

There's something in his voice, the way he says it, that makes her feel like the worst person in the world. "Except me, the heartless bitch, right?"

He shakes his head. "That's not what I said. Look, I just know that once you see them, once they see you, nothing else will matter. The past is the past. It's gone, you know? It doesn't matter anymore." He pauses. "All we have is now. Right now."

Her eyes go back to the clock. She stares at it, and it's not long before the number changes again.

Another minute has passed.

She closes her eyes as water starts to fill them. She doesn't want to cry. Not now. Not ever. Crying's stupid. It never changes anything.

There's no way to change any of it.

There's not a single thing they can do.

It's done.

Over.

Soon.

Really soon.

Too soon.

Panic rises up as her heart races. "Can you pull over, please?"

He looks at her, his eyes now filled with concern. "What's wrong?"

"I need some air. Now! Just pull over!"

He does as she says. She gets out and stumbles across the asphalt, the heat rising up, almost suffocating her. She makes her way to the grassy field as she tries to catch her breath. She feels Vince trying to put his arm around her. Trying to offer support or affection or something, but she pushes him away.

"Let me breathe," she gasps.

"Em, you're scaring me."

She stops and stands up straight and tall, her breaths coming fast. "Well, join the freaking club." And then, her anger dissolves as she crosses her arms over her chest. "Oh my God, Vince, I'm so scared. What are we going to do? I don't want to die. Maybe I'd convinced myself that I did. Told myself there wasn't anything to live for. But, yesterday and today, the world's proven me wrong. And now, I'm supposed to give it all up?"

She turns her back to Vince and shouts up at the sky. "Well, I don't want to!"

Tears sting her eyes, and she tries to stop them, but it's useless. It's not fair, her thoughts whisper over and over again. How can it be over now, when she's getting to the best part?

She loves him. And he loves her. It's good and right and true, but there's too much going on to rejoice in any of that. All she feels is an ever-increasing terror about what comes next, and anger at having to go way too soon.

"Love shouldn't end," she whispers as he gently spins her around to face him again.

He takes one of her hands and places it over his heart as he leans down to kiss her forehead. "Who says it has to?"

It's so sweet and tender, more tears fall. Emerson falls, too, right into Vince's arms, and he is there. Always there. Thank God.

It seems there's nothing to do but let go and give in. And with that thought, she cries even harder.

*TAKE WHAT'S* given
and accept it.
Deal with it.
Maybe even
learn to embrace it.

That's what
they say.

When life is dark
and ugly.
When hunger is
your only friend.
When every minute
feels like an hour.

That's when it's
easy to accept it.
Deal with it.
Maybe even embrace it.

Because through it all
you don't feel worthy
of anything else.

But now life is
palace-rose pink
with silver streaks.
There is hope,
happiness,
and endless possibility.

You've tasted the
macaron of life
and it is sweet.

Maybe you don't
deserve it.

But maybe you do.

All you want
is the chance
to find out.

Accept your fate?
Deal with it?
Embrace it?

Before,
it was easy.

Now
it feels
completely
impossible.

WITH NOTHING else to do, Carl sits at the patio table, eating cookies. Rhonda is pacing again. She's tried to stay positive and upbeat.

"They'll be back soon," she must have said a dozen times.

Now the poor woman looks pale. Frightened. She is worried sick. Of course, she doesn't burden Carl with that worry, but he can see it, all over her face.

"Why don't you sit down," Carl says. He points to the plate of Nilla Wafers. "Have a cookie. They're really good."

"I shouldn't have let them go," she mutters. "Why wasn't he over here, first thing this morning, so it wasn't an issue? Frankie woke up and wondered why he hadn't come by to say good-bye." She looks at Carl. "You wanna know why? Because people are assholes sometimes, that's why."

"By *he*, you mean her father?" Carl asks.

"Yes. She felt like she should go and see him. That's the problem with Frankie. She's so damn thoughtful all the time."

He chuckles. "That's a problem, all right. So wait, you said Frankie's dad isn't Paige's dad?"

She stops pacing and looks at Carl. "That's correct."

"Come on," he says, scooting a chair out for her. "Take a seat."

She hesitates a moment, but does as he asks. Once she's

seated, she stares at the plate of cookies for a long time. She reaches out and fiddles with one as she talks. "Carl, what you don't know about me is that I've been an awful mother."

"No. I don't believe that."

"It's true, though." Her eyes, starting to fill with tears, meet his. Then she whispers, "What if they're not coming back?"

"What do you mean?"

She tries to blink the tears back. "I mean, what if they didn't want to spend the last hours with me? I'll be here, all alone. My three girls, three darling daughters, gone. Spending their last day somewhere else. Anywhere else. Away from their horrible mother."

"Don't talk like that," Carl says. "There's still time." He smiles. "Besides, if they don't come back, you won't be alone. You'll be stuck with me, I'm afraid."

"What a mess," she says. "Never in a million years would I have pictured the last day like this."

"Life is full of surprises, I guess," Carl says, picking up another cookie and eating it.

"Do you have any regrets?" she asks. "Anything you'd do differently?"

He sighs as he leans back in his chair. "Of course. Who doesn't?"

"Yeah. I just wish I didn't have so many." She takes a drink of water. "I'd make you a nice, long list, but we don't have enough time. A lot of them involve Emerson, though. God knows she wasn't an easy child, but I should have handled things better."

"I don't have kids, but I've always believed being a parent must be the hardest job there is."

"Was that by choice?" she asks. "Not having kids, I mean?"

He shakes his head. "No. It wasn't meant to be. We almost adopted a baby. A little boy. But, at the last second, the mother changed her mind. It broke my wife's heart. She didn't want to put herself through that again."

"Oh no. I'm so sorry."

He waves his hand. "Nah. Don't be. It was probably for the best. I can't imagine how hard it must be, thinking about your kids as the time gets closer. Wanting to protect them, like you've always done, but not being able to do so."

Rhonda bows her head, and Carl watches as tears fall down her face. He reaches out and touches her hand. "Hey. Don't cry. I'm sorry if I said something wrong."

She sniffles. "The thing is, I haven't always protected them. I really am a terrible mother. I chose my boyfriend over my daughter. I couldn't stand how she was acting. The way they fought, all the time. So, I kicked her out. Told her she had to go live with her dad."

"You probably did the best you could at the time," Carl says.

She wipes the tears away with her thumbs. "No. I should have done better. She deserved better." She stands up. Starts pacing again.

There is so much regret hanging from this woman, and Carl wishes he could just cut it away for her. All those people he helped and had fun with, giving them something they wished for, and here is this woman, who's been so kind, and he can't do a single thing for her.

Or . . . can he?

EMERSON CRIED for a long time, there in the field, next to the freeway. A car would drive by every once in a while. A couple of them honked. But Vince and Emerson stood there, beneath the clear blue sky, in each other's arms, ignoring all of it.

Eventually, the tears dried up. She was spent. Exhausted beyond words. Vince helped her to the car. Put her seat in the reclining position. She crawled in, closed her eyes, and slept.

When she wakes, the first thing she does is glance at the clock. "Vince, why'd you let me sleep so long?"

"Trust me, you needed it."

"But I wasted precious time." She feels like she might start crying again, although she doesn't want to. Because sadness is not very helpful right now.

When she realizes they aren't moving, she reaches over and pops her seat up. "Where are we?"

"Well, I decided we needed something to eat. When I saw the Shari's sign from the freeway, and noticed cars parked out front, I thought we could check it out."

"You think it's open?"

"I don't know. But we're about to find out."

"Why would it be open, though?" she asks.

"Maybe the same reason the karaoke place was open? To help people somehow? Come on, let's go."

In some ways, it seems like a silly thing to do, when time is ticking away. But she can't deny it—she's hungry.

As they walk to the front door, she looks at the signs, all over the windows. Most of them are advertising pie.

Pie!

"Oh my God, I want pie," she says out loud.

Vince laughs. "What about that cheeseburger we were talking about earlier?"

"That, too. I know, let's order the entire menu. Everything. We have enough money, right?"

"Probably."

"Our last meal will be all eighty-seven items on the Shari's menu. Doesn't that sound awesome?"

"Wait. Have you actually counted how many things are on the menu?" Vince asks as he opens the front door and holds it for her.

"Remember that one time we went and ordered two waters and split a plate of french fries?"

"Yeah."

"I can't believe you didn't notice me counting everything on the menu."

He steps behind her, into the waiting area. "You're joking."

"Yes. I'm joking. Still, we're ordering everything. Deal?"

Before Vince can reply, an old man with glasses, lots of age spots, and hardly any hair stands up from a long table off to the side that's filled with people. Fifteen to twenty people, Emerson guesses.

The old man waves. Smiles. "Oh, good, two more! Please,

come in. We'll get you a couple of chairs. Don't worry, we haven't started yet. We're glad you're able to join us."

Vince and Emerson look at each other, not sure what to do. A couple of people from the group have sprung into action and gathered up two more chairs. Everyone scoots over and back, to make room.

"It's all right," the old man says. "Don't be frightened. We're absolutely thrilled you're here. You're so young, too. Most of us skeptics are in the over-sixty crowd. It'll be great to hear what you have to say."

Vince looks at Emerson again, and as he does, he glances quickly toward the door. Like he's telling her they should make a run for it. But Emerson doesn't want to go. The word *skeptics* has made her curious. She moves toward the empty chairs, so Vince follows. As they approach the table, she sees some people have ordered food.

"I'm Burt," the old guy says. "I'm the organizer of this meeting. And you are?"

"I'm Vince, and this is Emerson."

As they take their seats, Emerson says, "We've been traveling and we're really hungry. Would it be possible to order some food?"

"Of course," a middle-aged man with a big belly says as he stands up. "I'm Tom, the manager here, and I'm happy to get you something to eat. It'll just be a sandwich and some potato chips. Hope that's all right?"

"That sounds great," Vince says at the same time Emerson asks, "Do you have any pie?"

Vince turns and looks at her, his eyebrows high, like he's surprised by her question. She just shrugs her shoulders.

"We have one pie left," Tom says. "I'm afraid it's not very exciting: pumpkin. But I have some whipped cream to go with it."

Emerson leans back and smiles. "Perfect."

Tom returns her smile and then leaves the table, heading back toward the kitchen.

"So, how did you hear about us?" Burt asks.

"Uh, well," Vince says, "to be honest, we don't know much. We just, uh, we—"

Emerson can tell he's struggling, so she cuts in. "We heard some people talking about you in downtown Portland. And we were curious, you know?"

This seems to satisfy Burt. He nods. "Ah. Well, good. I'm glad to hear the measures we took to get the word out actually worked. Did you bring any evidence along with you?"

Emerson narrows her eyes. "Evidence?"

"Yes," Burt says. "Evidence that suggests this asteroid thing is all a giant, horrible hoax."

Emerson's mouth drops open for a moment, before she comes to her senses and responds. "No, sorry. We don't have any evidence. But we'd love to hear what you have to say."

Burt nods. "Yes. That's why we're all here. So let's get started, shall we?"

EMERSON IS trying to wrap her head around this. These people are here because they think the whole thing has been made up?

As in, a big, fat lie?

It's so bizarre, and part of her thinks maybe they should have run the other way when they had the chance. But another part of her is curious and really wants to hear what they have to say.

"First of all," a lady sitting next to Burt says, "I think we should share the reasons why we believe the government would do this to us. Why they would leak a fake disaster and create a crisis where none existed before? And then after that, we can share the evidence we've discovered."

"Sounds good to me," Burt says. "Let's go around the table, and hear what you each have to say. Please tell us your name before you speak."

Emerson listens intently as each person gives a reason.

"I'm Joe. They hate ninety-nine percent of us. It's that simple."

"Name's Bud. They want us to wake up and smell the coffee. The world was going to hell in a handbasket, and no one seemed to give a damn. So they're giving us a wake-up call like nothing we've seen before."

"Hello. I'm Shirley. And yes, I agree with Bud. I think they were frightened about where our nation was headed, and they simply didn't know what else to do."

"My name is Gloria. I have a different theory from a lot of you. I think it's real, but I believe they've figured out a way to prevent it from happening, and haven't told us yet. I think they want to take us as close to the estimated time of impact as possible. Really shake things up so when it's all over, our country won't be as divided as it once was."

"I'm David. Interesting theory. Personally, I think they wanted to get rid of as many of us as they could. And it worked, didn't it? I bet when it's over, some will come home, but many will stay where they are. Most of those who've left have probably begun the process of starting over. Lots of people talk about how we need free health care and free education. Well, once they find it in other countries, why would they want to come back here?"

It's Vince's turn now. He looks around the table, like he's trying to think of what to say. The words come out slowly. "I'm Vince. I'm thinking maybe they wanted to teach us a lesson."

An old lady with pure white hair who hasn't spoken yet leans forward, across the table. "But, what kind of lesson, exactly?"

"I don't know," Vince replies. "Maybe to remind us of what's really important in life? Like, if you've got your health and your family, you've got a lot, and you should be thankful for that. They say money is the root of all evil, and it seems like our society had hit an all-time high with its greed."

"The problem with that theory, however," Bud says, "is that the government is the greediest of them all. How does this help them in the end?"

Vince just shrugs his shoulders and looks at Emerson. Everyone else does the same, since it's her turn now.

"Can I ask a question?" she says.

"Of course," Burt replies. "Ask away."

"Whatever the reason for this 'hoax,' as you call it, doesn't it all seem a little extreme? I mean, couldn't they have come up with something less terrifying? Less tragic, maybe?"

"We must remember, wars have been started over much less," a tiny old man says at the opposite end of the table. "And what are wars, if not extreme, terrifying, and tragic?"

No one says anything as they take that in. A few people nod their heads in agreement. Just then, Tom returns, carrying two large plates of food. He sets the plates in front of Emerson and Vince. "There are glasses and pitchers of water there, on the table." He points. "Help yourselves. I'll be right back with your pie."

"Thank you," Emerson and Vince say simultaneously.

"So, what's your theory?" the old lady asks, looking at Emerson. "Do you have one?"

Emerson has already picked up her sandwich and taken a bite. It's ham and cheese on toasted white bread, and it's delicious. She finishes chewing and then says, "Maybe they're punishing us. Maybe this is how they say—stop being assholes, because ultimately, assholes don't end up with the good stuff. They get what they deserve. So stop wanting your way, all the time. Stop fighting all the freaking time. Try to get along with one another. I mean, have you seen the headlines of the paper recently? There's this one machine downtown that's broken, and it's easy to get a free paper . . ."

Her voice trails off as she realizes she's just admitted to stealing the newspaper. She picks up a chip, pops it in her mouth, and looks at Vince. "No one gets along anymore. What's with all the school shootings? The mall shootings? And terror threats, every day practically, and everywhere. Most days, doesn't it seem like the world has gone insane? So, they decided to punish us. Give us a good, hard kick. And suddenly, we're forced to get along, right? Look at all of us, sitting here." She leans in. "I mean, really. Would you all have been so friendly to us under any other circumstances?"

A couple of the people at the table squirm slightly.

"Punishing us," a woman with short red hair says. "Interesting. I'd never thought of it like that before, but it makes sense. I'm April, by the way."

Emerson eats another chip and keeps talking. "My friend Vince here, he's a good guy. He's always looking out for people. But me? I mostly keep to myself if I can. I don't trust other people, generally. In my mind, everyone's bad until I get proof otherwise. But not Vince. He wants to bring out the best in everyone. Do you know how we've spent the last twenty-four hours? Helping people. That's what he wanted to do. If only the rest of the world were like that, you know?"

Vince sets his sandwich down and reaches over and rubs Emerson's back. She smiles over at him as she takes another bite of her sandwich.

Tom appears with the plates of pumpkin pie and sets them on the table before he returns to his seat.

"All right," Burt says. "Clearly, there are more than enough theories to go around as to why they'd do this to us. The more we talk about it, the more it seems like it really could be an evil, elaborate plan."

Emerson is a bit surprised when she finds herself nodding her head in agreement.

"So, just to play the devil's advocate," Vince says. "We've all heard the theory that a huge asteroid is what killed off the dinosaurs millions of years ago. What's not to say that it really is happening? That tonight will be the end for all of us?"

"Well," Burt says, "that's where the evidence comes in. Are we ready to present what we have to the group?"

Everyone nods.

Vince and Emerson look at each other, like they can't believe what they have accidentally stepped into. And then, still hungry, they go back to eating.

"THE FIRST thing to examine," Burt says, "is the state of the economy at the time we got word of the asteroid."

"I had the exact same thought," Tom says. "Unemployment rates had been going up for months. Businesses were shutting their doors right and left. Then, the stock market crashed and it was unlike anything we've seen since the Great Depression. It was twenty-four hours of absolute chaos. The economy was in a tailspin."

"Shortly thereafter," Burt says, "the announcement of the impending disaster hit the airwaves. Highly suspect, don't you agree?"

Emerson glances around the table as, once again, everyone nods their heads.

The woman with the red hair, April, clears her throat, and all eyes turn to her. She's not as old as most of the others. Forty, maybe. Intelligent-looking. "If they'd been waiting for the right time to pull the trigger, so to speak, they found it." She leans in. "But I have something very interesting that you're not going to believe."

The table gets very quiet. Emerson stops chewing and sets her sandwich down on the plate.

"Did you ever wonder," April continues, "why the only

interviews they showed in the days immediately following the announcement were with the same two astronomers?"

"I never thought about it, actually," Joe says.

"I have a friend at the Pentagon," April says. "I spoke with him a few days ago. Unlike many others, he did not leave the country. It seemed strange to me, so I asked him straight-out, to tell me what he knows. He was reluctant to do so at first. But I pressed him, and I kept pressing him. I said, in just a few days, everyone is going to find out the truth anyway. One way or the other, the truth will be revealed. What does it hurt to tell me now?"

Emerson is on the edge of her seat as she listens to this lady talk about secrets at the Pentagon. She feels Vince's hand reach under the table to find hers, and it makes her relax a little bit.

April folds her hands and puts them on the table in front of her. She speaks slowly. Carefully. "There was an astronomy conference right before the announcement of the asteroid. Apparently, top experts from around the world, who were at this conference, are now locked away in a secret location."

"How convenient," Burt says.

"Yes," April says. "He wouldn't tell me where they are, and when I asked him why they've done that, he said the go-to answer is for research purposes. That, of course, government officials want to do everything in their power to see if they can find a way to stop the tragedy from occurring." She pauses. "But I asked him, why do I get the feeling that the go-to answer isn't the real answer? The honest answer?"

"Because it's not," Bud says. "Isn't that right?"

April leans back. "That's all I could get out of him. He said he'd told me far more than he should have."

"What do you think?" Burt asks. "What do your instincts tell you, April? Surely you must have had a gut response after you hung up the phone."

"I think he was lying through his teeth," April says. "My theory? They've gathered up all of the experts and locked them away so none of them can cry foul. They bought off a couple of others who would respond to questions and tell the world the lies that our government has meticulously created."

"God," Emerson whispers. "This is sick."

Vince squeezes her hand, as if trying to reassure her.

"But what about cell and Internet service going out?" Gloria asks. "The shortage of gasoline? Are you saying that's all been staged?"

"Of course," Joe says. "They've gone to great lengths to make it look real. And don't you find it strange that we still have electricity? It doesn't make sense."

The look on Gloria's face tells Emerson she is feeling very confused, and Emerson wants to tell her she's not the only one. Instead, she asks the question that's been bouncing around inside her head for the past few minutes. "So, when we don't blow up, what happens then? What will they say about it all?"

"They'll tell us they found a way to prevent it," Tom says. "The United States government will come out smelling like a fresh load of laundry. They'll make us believe that the team of experts solved the problem in the nick of time. Trust me, they'll have an answer for everything."

"Yes. The US government will be the world's hero," April says. "Just the way they like it. They'll tell us things need to be different. That we have a second chance at life, and we'd better do everything we can not to mess things up this time around."

"They'll expect us to pay the piper, that's for sure," Joe says.

Emerson lets go of Vince's hand and picks up the small plate with the piece of pie and starts eating. She tells herself to savor every bite, in case it's the last piece of pie she'll ever have. But she can't deny it—where there was certainty before, that this would be her last day, doubt has crept in.

There are so many questions, but she knows, right now, no one really has any answers. She tells herself to enjoy the pumpkin pie. It's smooth and creamy, with just the right amount of spices. The whipped cream is rich and sweet.

It tastes so good. She keeps her mind focused on the delicious dessert. After all, it's about the only thing that makes any sense right now.

**THERE WERE** days and nights
they didn't eat anything
and she thought of a family,
sitting down for dinner,
kids being loud and obnoxious,
Father taking his place
without so much as a thanks,
and Mother, sitting down,
praying it's good enough,
hoping they eat it,
wiping her bangs from her eyes
and smiling through it all.

It was time to eat, but
they had other things
on their minds, too,
as they gathered
after a stressful day
of meetings, of phone calls,
of endless emails, and
of tests and tattling.

Soon, their stomachs would be
full and they would turn on
the television, open the books,
surf the Internet, and
eat a cookie or two or five.

As her stomach growled,
she wished cookies were provided
free of charge like water
from a drinking fountain,
and she wished people
appreciated everyone
and everything
a little more.

THE COOKIES are gone. Carl sits at the table on the patio and waits for Rhonda to return. He's not sure why he didn't think of it before. Perhaps it was the concussion. He told his wife to check with neighbors, to see if there were any cars not being used or some left behind, gassed up and ready to go. Why shouldn't they do the same?

He told Rhonda they should go around the cul-de-sac and see what they could find. She insisted that she go by herself because he shouldn't exert himself too much yet. He'd argued at first, but eventually, he agreed to stay on the patio and wait for her.

When the sliding door opens, he turns around, expecting to see Rhonda, but it's not her.

"Who are you?" the man asks.

"I'm Carl," he says as he stands up and extends a hand. "A friend of Rhonda's. And you are?"

The man takes his hand and shakes it, though he seems to do it rather reluctantly. "I'm James, her ex-husband. Frankie and Emerson's father. So, where is she?"

"Checking the neighborhood for an available car. We were getting really worried about Frankie and Paige."

Just then, Frankie appears, carrying a sleeping Paige in her arms. "Where's my mom?"

"I'll go find her," James says. "Be right back."

"I'm gonna put Paige down," Frankie says.

"All right," Carl says. "Your mom will be so happy to have you home."

"It wasn't my fault we took so long," Frankie explains. "While we were inside, talking to my dad, someone stole our car. When we walked out, it was just . . . gone. Dad couldn't leave right away, because his sister, my aunt Becky, was on her way over to say good-bye with her two kids."

"What an ordeal," Carl says. He waves his hand. "Go ahead and put your sister to bed. I'll help get your mom up to speed."

She turns around and heads back inside, and Carl follows behind her. Frankie walks toward the stairs while Carl makes his way to the front door. Just as he's about to go outside, the door opens. He steps back so James and Rhonda can come in.

"They're home!" Rhonda tells Carl. "Can you believe it? I'm so relieved I could cry."

"Yes," Carl says. "It's great news. Although your car got stolen. Did he tell you?"

"Isn't it crazy?" Rhonda says. "I guess cars with fuel are a hot commodity right now. It's okay. My babies are home and that's all that really matters."

Carl gulps, because obviously, she's forgotten he still needs a ride. He's going to have to ask James, and he hates the idea of that when he doesn't even know him.

When Frankie returns, she asks her dad, "Did you tell her? What we're going to do?"

Rhonda looks back and forth, from one to the other. "What do you mean? Do what?"

"Frankie asked if I'd take her downtown to look for her sister some more," James says. "I told her I would."

Rhonda turns to Frankie. "Oh no. Honey, I don't think that's a good idea. As the time gets closer, I'm afraid things may get crazy. It might be dangerous downtown."

Frankie crosses her arms. "Which is exactly why we need to find Emerson. She should be here. With us. Don't you get it? Don't you care?"

"Of course I care. I just think we should give this some thought. I mean, is this really how you want to spend your last few hours?"

"Mom," Frankie says. "I can't believe you are saying this. She's my sister. There's nothing more important than finding her. Besides, what else are we going to do? Sit around here and watch some poor guy on the news do a countdown for us? Jesus, this isn't like New Year's Eve, you know?"

Before Rhonda can respond, Carl speaks up. "Maybe we should all go. We can cover more ground that way."

Rhonda considers this idea before she looks at her ex-husband and says, "Yes. If you two are insisting on going, I don't want to stay here."

"I'm happy to help you," Carl says. "Then I wonder if you might be willing to give me a ride home after that? I know it's asking a lot, but I've been trying to get home since yesterday and—"

"Oh my goodness, Carl, I'm so sorry," Rhonda says. "Of course you want to get home. I'm afraid I didn't find any cars available at the neighbors' houses."

Carl tries to hide his disappointment. "That's all right. I'll help you and then you can return the favor, how's that sound? We'll find her. I have a good feeling."

"Is there anything to eat?" Frankie asks. "I'm starving. And if we wake up Paige, she's going to be, too."

Rhonda turns to Carl. "While I get Paige, would you mind rounding up snacks and bottles of water? Apples from the backyard, crackers, whatever else you can find. I think there's a few granola bars in the cupboard." She turns back to Frankie. "When we get back, there's a frozen lasagna I can pop in the oven."

"That's what we're having for our last meal?" Frankie asks. "Frozen lasagna?"

Rhonda laughs nervously. "Well, you know me. A cook I am not. Why should that change now?"

"THAT WAS . . ." Vince turns on the car as Emerson buckles up.

"Intense?" Emerson adds. "Strange? Sort of convincing?"

He looks over at her. "Are you convinced?"

"I don't know. I don't know what to think. To believe. All I know is yesterday I wanted pumpkin pie, and today I got pumpkin pie. The rest I'm still trying to process."

Vince merges onto the freeway. "I can't believe they'd do that. Stage a huge disaster like this."

"But if they wanted to press the reset button, what an incredible way to do it, right?" Emerson says as she looks out the window. Their car is only one of three she can see all the way up the interstate. It's weird. Eerie.

"But like you said," Vince says, "it's so extreme."

"And also maybe a little brilliant." Vince looks over at her like she's crazy. "Think about it. If we're still alive tonight at midnight, people will be dancing in the streets. They won't care about anything else except for one thing."

"That we're alive," Vince says.

"Exactly."

"But will that feeling last? Like, what happens a few months from now, when the economy is worse than ever and people still can't find work?"

"We all move to Ireland?" Emerson says in a bad Irish accent.

Vince nods and tries his best to sound Irish as well. "There are only two kinds of people in the world: the Irish and those who wish they were."

Emerson laughs. "You sound like the leprechaun in the Lucky Charms commercial."

"Magically delicious," he sings.

She leans over and kisses him on the cheek. "You're so cute."

"You only like me for my awesome car."

"Yep. And all that cash in your wallet we still haven't managed to spend." Emerson gasps as her hand flies to her mouth. "Oh no. If it's all a lie, that guy . . . what's his name?"

"Carl."

"Yeah, Carl. If it's a lie, he died for nothing."

"Well, keep in mind, it's still a big if."

"You don't believe it?"

"Don't get me wrong. I *want* to believe it. Remember, I asked you earlier, what if it's all a big mistake, didn't I? But I guess I have a hard time imagining anyone, even the US government, pulling off something as big as this. Come on, think about it. They couldn't have managed to find all the astronomers, could they? Someone would have come forward and called them on it if it wasn't true. Don't you think?"

Emerson chews on her lip. "Unless the astronomers are scared for some reason."

"Okay, so you need to tell me what exit to take."

She looks at him. "What? What are you talking about?"

"To get to your house. What exit? You know the name of it, right?"

"We're still going?"

He reaches his hand over and squeezes her knee. "Yes, we're still going. We have to assume the worst, I think. Make sure nothing is left undone."

She doesn't say anything.

"It's going to be okay, Em. I'll be right there with you."

"I wish I could be as sure as you are, but whatever. We take the Terwilliger exit."

"Got it. Thanks."

They're quiet for a few minutes.

"Vince?"

"Yeah?"

"What if it doesn't happen? Like, what will we do then? Do we go back on the streets?"

Vince groans. "That thought right there? It makes my stomach hurt." He turns and looks at her for a second. "We'd have to figure something else out. I don't want to go back to that. Do you?"

"Hey, we have a car now," Emerson says. "We could live right here!"

"Don't you think Jackie might want it back?" Vince asks.

"Maybe not. Let's pretend she gives it to us. It's more fun that way."

"Okay, so maybe we could sell it," Vince says. "Take the money and find us a little place to rent. Get some help and study for our GEDs. Because I'm not kidding. I don't want to go back to that life. If I've learned anything these past twenty-four hours, it's that what we had wasn't much of a life at all."

"We did the best we could," Emerson says.

"You're right. We did. But I feel like now, we can do so much better. Here's a question for you. If your mom asked you to move back in with her, would you say yes?"

"She wouldn't do that."

"She might."

"Well, I can't even imagine that happening, so there's no use talking about it."

"Here we go," he says, pointing to the sign that says TERWILLIGER.

"Great," she replies. "Now *my* stomach hurts."

"IT'S NICE," Vince says when they pull up across the street from her house.

Emerson studies the old green house with black trim. As she does, she takes a deep breath in an effort to calm herself down as she thinks about seeing the people behind the front door. "Charming. That's what my mom said when we moved here. After my parents divorced. To me it just seemed old and run-down. You should hear the way the stairs creak. Sneaking out was such a bitch. I had it down to a science, where to walk and which steps to skip."

"Where'd you go when you snuck out?"

"Oh, you know. Parties, mostly."

Vince narrows his eyes. "What about dates?"

"Dates?"

"Yeah, you know, dinner and a movie, where you make out in the back row for two solid hours."

"Oh no. I didn't really have any dates. Why? Is that what you did when you snuck out?"

He laughs as he puts his hands to his chest. "Me? No way. I was a good boy."

"Right. And cheeseburgers grow on trees."

He leans in and kisses her. Holds her face in his hands like he's holding a delicate Fabergé egg. "None of that really matters now, right?"

"Right." She kisses him again. "I just wish . . ."

"What?"

"I wish I could keep you."

He stares into her eyes and there is no doubt in her mind he means it when he says, "I wish you would."

The whole conversation has a soothing effect on her. Maybe everything will be okay, after all. She tells herself to hold on to that thought.

They kiss one more time before he pulls away and says, "You ready?"

She takes another deep breath. "Not at all. But who cares? We're here."

They get out and Emerson walks slowly toward the front door, trying to peer into the front window as she goes. The curtains are open, but she doesn't see anyone.

"I'll let you do the honors," Vince says, stepping aside so Emerson can knock. And that's what she does, before she can think too hard about it and change her mind.

"My heart is beating so fast right now," she whispers.

"I know; I can hear it."

She looks at him, shocked. "Can you really?"

He smiles and shakes his head. She sticks her tongue out at him.

When no one comes to the door, she knocks again, louder this time. But again, no one answers.

Vince tries the doorknob. It's locked. "Well, this sucks."

Emerson feels relief mixed with a little disappointment. "What do you want to do now?"

"Is there anywhere else they might be?"

"Obviously, they went somewhere, but I'm not sure I'd even know where to look. My mom's mother is dead and her dad lives in the South. They weren't very close, so I don't think they would have gone there. I don't remember much about Kenny's family."

"Kenny?" Vince asks.

"My mom's boyfriend. Or maybe husband by now? Who knows?"

"Oh, that's right. Sorry, I forgot his name. What about your dad? I think we should go to his house. It'd be good for you to see him, and maybe he knows where your mom is."

"Yeah. Maybe. Or we could wait here. See if she comes back?"

"Nah, I think we should go. See if we can find your dad."

Emerson lets out a sigh as she cuddles up close to him. She kisses his neck. "Maybe we should stop worrying about all of them and go somewhere special. Just the two of us. Maybe watch the sun set?"

He kisses the top of her head and then runs down the steps, pulling on her arm as he goes. "Hold that thought. We still have a couple more hours of daylight. In the meantime, the search continues. Come on."

She stumbles down the front steps. "You are such a pain in the ass sometimes."

"What happened to, 'You're a good man, Charlie Brown'?"

"I take it back. All the nice things I've ever said about you, I take them back."

He pulls her to him. "You love me and you know it."

She looks in his beautiful brown eyes and feels herself melting. "Fine. You're right. I do."

He gently strokes her hair. "I'm sorry they're not here, Em."

She kisses him. "I know."

"But we're gonna find them," he says, turning toward the car. "I promise."

WHEN THEY find no one home at Emerson's dad's house, they take a seat on the porch swing.

"I love these things," Vince says. "If I lived here, I don't think I'd do anything else but just sit here and swing."

As they sway back and forth, gently, Emerson sinks down and puts her head on Vince's shoulder. "You'd get so bored."

"Not if I had a nice guitar to play." He kisses the top of her head. "Or a cute girl to cuddle with."

"Hey, you know what?" Emerson sits up straight. "My dad has a guitar. We should see if we can get inside and find it. It'd be like old times. Did you try the doorknob?"

"Yeah. It's locked."

"Let's go around back," Emerson says. "He's really bad about keeping that door locked."

There's a fence along the backyard, but the gate is open. They make their way to the small patio and the door that leads into the laundry room. When Emerson tries the handle, it turns easily. Before she walks in, she looks at Vince. "If he comes home and finds us in here, I hope he doesn't get mad."

"Just tell him you had to pee really bad."

"Right. And I decided to play the guitar to entertain myself while I did my business?"

"No, we'll throw it down on the floor and pretend we didn't have anything to do with it."

"That's some plan, Mr. Goofball."

"Takes one to know one."

They walk through the laundry room and into the small kitchen, where the faint smell of bacon lingers. She leads him into the dining room and then toward the stairs by the front door. They stop and glance around the family room, which is sparse, with just a sofa, love seat, a television, and the old juke-box in a corner.

"He used to keep the guitar in his bedroom, so I'm guessing that's where it is," Emerson says.

"You go ahead," Vince says. "I'll stay down here and keep watch."

"So, what, you gonna give me a signal if he pulls up in the driveway or something?"

"Yeah, I'll whistle." He puts his fingers in his mouth and gives a catcall. "How's that?"

"Or you could just yell, 'He's home!'"

He laughs. "That'd probably work, too."

Emerson climbs the old wooden stairs, watching as Vince takes a seat on the sofa. When she gets to the top of the stairs, she automatically heads to the room that she and her sister shared when they came to visit. The room that became hers when she moved in after her mom kicked her out. She decides she wants to see it. She's curious. Are there still two beds? Did her sister change anything about it when Emerson didn't come back? What about all the clothes she left behind?

When she opens the door, she gasps.

Whatever she might have expected, it wasn't this.

**NOTES HUNG** all over the room.

On pink paper,
blue paper,
green paper,
purple paper.

A rainbow of notes.
Each with a few words.
On every wall.

Where are you?
Why'd you go?
I miss you.
I need you.
I love you.
Please come back.
They love you, too.
They miss you, too.
I want you to come home.
Why don't you call me?
Please talk to me.
I'm here.

Where are you?
Are you cold?
Are you hungry?
Are you alive?

Beyond the notes,
in the closet,
all of Emerson's clothes.
Her shoes.
Her stuff.

Nothing's been moved.

Frankie was waiting for
her to come back.

All this time.
Waiting.

CARL WISHES time would slow down. Or stop altogether. Anything but continue to pass at this incredibly fast pace.

"It'll be dark soon, I'm afraid," Carl says from the passenger seat of James's luxury sedan.

Carl, Rhonda, and Paige have been driving all over downtown while James and Frankie got out to walk around Waterfront Park. Rhonda didn't think it was a good idea for Carl to exert himself, so she took the wheel when James and her oldest daughter got out to look around on foot. She and Carl have stopped and asked a few people if they've seen Emerson, sharing her picture with them, but so far, no luck.

"Yeah, another thirty minutes and then I think it's time to give up the ghost," Rhonda says. "Wish I'd brought my last bottle of wine along. I could really use a drink about now."

The thought makes Carl's stomach churn. While she longs for a drink, he's thinking about how much he'd like a good dinner. Spaghetti, maybe. Or steak and a loaded baked potato. After all, he's only had an apple and some cookies since the pastries he and Jerry shared.

Rhonda turns a corner, pulls over, and parks the car. After she turns the engine off, she leans forward and rests her forehead on the steering wheel.

"Hey," Carl says. "You okay?"

She shakes her head, then looks out the window. "I'm tired and I want some dinner. I don't want to do this anymore. It's a waste of time."

"Maybe not," Carl says. "You just never know. She could be right around that corner up there."

"I feel like if she wanted to be found, she'd have made it easy for us. The fact that we've been looking this long and this hard, with hardly a trace of her, well, maybe we need to admit she doesn't want anything to do with us."

"Probably a hard thing to admit, yes?" Carl asks.

She looks at him with tears in her eyes. "Yes. But I think it's time. I just hope Frankie can forgive me. She really wanted to find her, in case you couldn't tell."

"And you?" Carl asks.

She stares out the window again. Presses her lips together, like she's thinking hard. "Of course I wanted to find her. She's my daughter."

"But?"

She looks at Carl and blinks a few times. "But, things were so much easier when she was little. I'm not sure I know how to be the kind of mother she needs now."

"Hm," Carl says, thinking about that. "My guess is today, the only kind of mother she needs is one who tells her that she is loved."

"I'm afraid she won't believe me," she says softly. "Ever heard that old saying, 'Actions speak louder than words'?"

When Paige starts babbling about something, Rhonda turns around and smiles. "Hey there, sweet pea. You eat all your crackers?" She grabs the sippy cup sitting in the drink carrier, reaches back, and hands it to her. "Here's some water."

"Tank you," Paige says before she puts the cup to her lips and drinks.

"See how easy it is with little ones?" Rhonda says when she turns back around.

It confuses him, this mention of the word *easy* again. Who ever said parenting was supposed to be easy? He quickly thinks back to his teen years and realizes there's nothing easy about that, either.

He supposes they're both in tough places, and he can't help but feel bad for each of them.

OVER THIRTY minutes of tears. Of sadness. Of hating herself so much for what she's done to her sister. Vince tried to console her when she came downstairs crying, but she pushed him away. Refused to tell him what had happened.

Now she sits at the far end of the sofa, unable to control the shuddering gasps that keep coming, even though the tears have finally stopped falling.

"Em, can I come sit by you now?" Vince asks from his spot at the other end. "Please?"

She feels so alone. Maybe more alone than she's ever felt. Suddenly, there's nothing more she wants than to feel Vince's arms around her. She looks at him and gives a little nod.

He's there in an instant, pulling her to him, whispering in her ear that it's all right. Everything's going to be all right.

"No," she whispers. "I don't think so."

"Do you want to go back to your mom's place? See if anyone's there?"

She shakes her head, hard. She's done looking for them. Knowing how much she's hurt her sister, she can hardly bear the thought of seeing her again. What could she say to make it better? What could she possibly say?

*Sorry* isn't good enough. A simple *sorry* doesn't make up for all those nights Frankie probably cried herself to sleep, imagining the worst.

God, how she must hate Emerson for what she's put her through. That single thought causes her eyes to fill with tears again.

"You know what?" Vince says. "I think we need to get you out of here. Obviously, I was wrong about coming here, and I'm so sorry. I thought it was the right thing to do, Em, and I hope you know I didn't mean to hurt you. I don't know what happened, what set you off, but I think we need to leave. Where do you want to go? I'll take you anywhere; just name the place."

She wants to go somewhere that can be theirs. All theirs, and no one else's. A place that feels like home. The home they've dreamed about during the hard days.

"I don't know," she says. "It's hard to think right now."

Vince pulls out Carl's wallet. "Remember this? We have money. Let's pretend it will get us anywhere we want to go. We took Jackie to Paris; now it's your turn. Don't think too hard, just listen to your gut. What's it say? Where does it want to go?"

She reaches for the wallet. Opens it. Looks at Carl's picture. Driver's license pictures usually aren't the best, but this one's good. He's not smiling a lot, but enough so he looks content. It's exactly how Emerson wants to feel. She wants to forget everyone and everything and feel like that.

"Here," she says, holding the license up to Vince. "Let's go to his house, and make it ours."

He gives her a funny look.

"He's gone," she explains. "Who knows what happened to his family. Why he was on that bridge. But his house will be empty, or he wouldn't have been there. We can pretend it's ours. Like when we were little. You must have played house, right? It'll be like that."

"It's probably a really nice place," Vince says.

"That's what I'm thinking," Emerson says. "Because it's in Lake Oswego." Her eyes get big. "Maybe it's on the lake. Wouldn't that be awesome?"

Vince shrugs. "Well, I guess we can go check it out. If you're sure there's nowhere else you want to go."

"I'm sure."

He stands up and helps her to her feet. "Do you want to talk about what you saw? What made you so sad?"

She shakes her head again. "No. I'm going to try and forget it. That's the only thing I can do now."

As they close the door behind them, Emerson thinks of all the colored notes, back in their room. She ripped them off the walls. Every single one. And then she gathered them up, one by one, in a neat little stack and threw them in the trash can.

She's broken her sister's heart. She knows that. And there's nothing she can do to fix it.

THEY'RE HEADING south again on I-5. The sun will be setting soon. Emerson leans her head against the window and wishes she could release the weight of the regret she feels.

"How do I let it go?" she asks, desperate to do just that.

"What?" Vince asks.

"I don't know. Everything I'm feeling bad about, basically."

"Can you be more specific?"

She sighs and sits up. "I hurt my sister. And I can't stop thinking about it. I guess I thought she didn't care very much." She pauses. "Or maybe I'm a selfish bitch and I didn't give her that much thought."

"Em, I know you're feeling bad, but the thing is? You can't change any of it. And really, if you could, would you want to? We wouldn't have met. I mean, think about that. These past twenty-four hours would have been completely different if we hadn't met. The Make-a-Wish-for-the-Apocalypse would not have been a thing."

She stares out her side window. The light is so pretty right now. There's a special warmth to the golden glow, as the sun makes its descent. It's practically hypnotic. She turns her thoughts to the people she and Vince have met recently.

Hayden. He nailed the Queen song.

Jackie and Phillip. A match made in make-believe Paris.

Kat. Backstabbing wench.

Kailee and Kendall, with their sweet dog, Teddy. Emerson's soul sisters in all things mother-related.

She can't deny it. Thinking about them makes her feel good. The fun they had. The wishes they granted.

Well, except for—

"Our Make-a-Wish-for-the-Apocalypse was awesome," Emerson says. "But I really could have done without that Kat girl."

Vince laughs. "Oh, come on. She was sixteen and never been kissed. She can die happy now."

"The kiss was good?"

"The kiss was excellent."

Emerson groans. "Do you enjoy stabbing me in the heart, Mr. Kiss-and-Tell?"

He laughs harder. "No, I mean, *for her*, the kiss was excellent. I gave her the best I had, but it was like a job, all right? It didn't mean anything."

"How come guys always say that?"

"What?"

She puts her hands up and makes air quotes. "'It didn't mean anything.' What a crock of shit."

"But it didn't. What do you want me to say to make you feel better? That she was a terrible kisser?"

"Was she?"

He reaches over and takes her hand. "Let me put it to you this way. Your kisses? Not even in the same league as hers. You are, like, getting your master's degree in kissing, while she's in fourth grade, chasing all the boys at recess, threatening to give them cooties."

Emerson smiles as she relaxes in her seat. "I like the sound of that. Master's degree in kissing."

He gives her hand a squeeze. "And you know, if you want to go for your doctorate, I'm happy to help."

She gives him a shove. "Oh my God, stop it with the cheese, would you? You should have quit while you were ahead."

Emerson feels him looking at her. She turns and meets his eyes. "What?"

He smiles. "I'm glad the Emerson I know and love, aka Ms. Tell-It-Like-It-Is is back, that's all."

She returns her eyes to the road and doesn't say anything for a moment. "I just can't let myself think about the stuff I wish I could change," she says. "You were right. Regret hurts."

"So, try to focus on the good."

"Once again, you say it like it's so easy."

"It's a lot easier than killing yourself with regret, isn't it?"

"Yeah. I guess so."

"From here on out, we need to stay focused on the right now."

She stares at the clock, remembering how it freaked her out, watching the minutes tick by. "Okay. I'll try."

## BIRDS DANCE
upon branches.

Mice scurry
in fields.

Spiders spin
across spaces.

No looking back
No looking ahead.

Each minute, each hour,
spent doing, spent living.

A means
of survival?

Or the way
it's meant to be?

Perhaps nature understands
what we do not.

It's not about
how we live.

Just that
we do.

Moment
by
sweet,

lovely

moment.

FRANKIE'S CURLED up in the corner of the backseat, crying. Paige has one of her hands in her sister's hair while she sucks the thumb of her other hand. Carl sits on the other side of the car seat, as James is behind the wheel again and Rhonda is in the passenger's seat.

"You need to pull it together, Frankie," Rhonda says as she turns around. "I will not spend these last couple of hours with you like this. I'm serious. You need to get it together because it's not fair to the rest of us."

"Hey, go easy on her, Rhonda," James says. "She's missing her sister. Worried about her, too."

"Dad, don't even try, all right?" Frankie says. "It won't do any good. Mom doesn't give a rat's ass."

"Watch it," Rhonda says. "Little ears and all."

"Okay, Carl," James says as he catches Carl's eyes in the rearview mirror. "Let's get you home, then I'll take these girls back to their house. Can you tell me where to go?"

*Home.* Carl's heart practically jumps out of his chest at just the mention of the word.

"I sure can."

VINCE AND Emerson pull up to the house on Edenberry Drive. Carl's house. It's smaller than most in the area, but really nice. Mocha colored with white trim. Pretty flowers in the beds, along with bushes of various sizes, and a beautiful Japanese maple in the front corner, next to the driveway.

As they came into town off the freeway, they spotted an elderly couple, strolling along a walking path. Vince stopped the car, got out, and asked if they might know how to get to Edenberry Drive, and they did. It so happened they weren't far from the street at all.

"Just take Westlake into the development," the old man said, "and you'll eventually come to it."

And so, here they are. But neither of them moves.

"This is weird, isn't it?" Emerson says.

"No, it's brilliant." He turns so he faces her. Leans in and kisses her. "Think about it. For the next couple of hours, it's only you and me. We'll have an entire house all to ourselves. Doing whatever we want."

He moves in to kiss her again, when she sees movement out of the corner of her eye. She turns to find a woman running toward the car, the front door of Carl's house wide open.

"Ummm," Emerson says.

"Who is that?" Vince asks.

"Like I'm supposed to know?"

Vince opens the door and gets out.

"Where is he?" the woman asks, running up to Vince, trying to peer past him, into the car.

"Who?" Vince asks as Emerson gets out.

"Carl," she says as she looks at Emerson. "He's with you two, right? That's why you're here?"

Emerson looks at Vince, feeling completely helpless. What should they say? Should they tell her about the man she's asking about, or let her continue to believe he'll be coming home eventually?

Vince turns back to the woman. "Are you his wife? Mrs. Ragsdale?"

"Yes."

"I'm sorry, he's not with us," Vince says. "He's not home, then?"

Emerson is watching the scene as if she's watching a movie. She has no idea where this is going, and she's incredibly anxious to find out.

Carl's wife looks like she's about ready to cry. "No. He's not here. I've been waiting for him to come home since yesterday."

Vince reaches into his back pocket. "We, um, found his wallet. On the street. And we wanted to return it to him." He reaches out and hands it to her.

"He told me he gave it away," she says, looking at the wallet with longing in her eyes. "His car, too." She returns her gaze to meet Vince's. "I don't know why he did that. He was trying to help people or something."

Emerson can't do it. She can't stand here and lie to this

woman. It's wrong. She has a right to know, doesn't she? That he'd been helping people, and that he was happy?

Really happy, it seemed to Emerson at the time.

"Actually," Emerson says as she steps toward Mrs. Ragsdale, "we didn't really find it. He gave it to us. We're the ones he wanted to help."

Mrs. Ragsdale shakes her head in confusion. "I don't understand."

Emerson looks at Vince, then back at Carl's wife. "Vince here, he didn't want to hurt you. But I think we should tell you the truth."

"Em, no," Vince says. "Don't."

"But she's his wife," Emerson says. "She's wasting time waiting for him. Worrying about him. Don't you think she should know?"

"No," Vince says firmly. "I really don't. I think—"

"Stop it!" Carl's wife screams. "Please. Stop! Tell me. I don't care what it is, I just want to know. I *have* to know."

Emerson takes another step forward and as she speaks, she does so gently. With kindness in her voice. As much kindness as she can find.

"We think he's dead," she says. "We met him on the Vista Bridge. He was about to jump when he spotted us. He came over and talked to us. Asked if there was anything he could do for us. When Vince said we could use some money, he gave us his wallet. And then he said he felt ready to say good-bye. At peace, is what he said."

Emerson watches. Waits for the woman to break down. To cry. To scream. Something. But she doesn't. A smile slowly spreads across her face. She closes her eyes and looks up at the sky. And then she starts laughing. She laughs and laughs.

It reminds Emerson of Carl—how he laughed when Vince asked him if he was sure he didn't want the wallet anymore.

"What?" Vince says. "What is it? What's so funny?"

"I called him," she explains. "I spoke to him. After he gave you the wallet. I can see now I called him in the nick of time. See, I was at my parents'. He didn't expect me to come home, but I did. I came home and he said he'd try his best to get here. So whatever's happened, I still have hope. I'm not going to give up on him."

Emerson shakes her head. "But why isn't he here yet? Even if he couldn't find a ride, he could have walked from downtown and been here by now. It doesn't make sense."

"Nothing makes much sense, does it?" she asks. "I mean, really, what do we know for sure except that right now, in this moment, we're standing here, breathing? The rest, who knows? Let's stop asking questions. Let's just stop trying to figure out everything and simply be happy we're here. What do you say?"

Emerson remembers Vince's words. *Stay focused on the right now.* She folds her arms across her chest and nods as Vince says, "Yeah. I agree. One hundred percent."

"Good," Mrs. Ragsdale says. "Now, would you like to tell me why you really came here?"

"Actually," Vince says, "I think we'd rather not. But please know we're glad you're here. And we really hope Carl gets home soon."

"Yes," Emerson says, thankful Vince didn't tell her they came to break into her house and pretend to live here for the next couple of hours. How awkward would that have been? "So, we should probably get going now. But tell Carl we said thanks. For everything. We're really glad we met him. Because of him, we've had an amazing twenty-four hours. He kind of changed our lives, if you want to know the truth."

"Are you sure you don't want to come inside?" Mrs. Ragsdale asks. "Wait and see if he shows up, so you can thank him yourself?"

Vince looks at Emerson, but she doesn't even have to think about it. "We're sure," she says. "But thanks for the offer. It was great to meet you."

"Wait," Carl's wife says. "I don't even know your names. I'm Trinity, by the way."

"I'm Vince."

"And I'm Emerson."

"Wonderful," Trinity says. "Well, I'm really glad I met you."

"Same here," Emerson says.

Vince waves. "I guess we'll say good-bye, then."

"'Bye," Emerson says before she turns and gets back in the car.

When Vince climbs in, he lets out a long breath. "Wow."

"Yeah," Emerson says.

Trinity stands there, holding the wallet to her heart, waving with her other hand. "She's nice," Vince says.

"I can totally see them together, can't you?" Emerson asks. "They're like two peas in a pod or however that saying goes."

"Like us?" Vince asks.

Emerson squeezes his leg as he puts the car in reverse. "No. Not like us. Come on, we're more exciting than that."

"Like two strings on a guitar?" Vince asks.

"Yeah. Or two fries on a Shari's plate."

They turn the corner, just as a luxury sedan is coming the other way.

"Or two stupid kids in a fancy BMW," Vince says with a grin. "Now there's an original one."

But she didn't hear him. Because she thought she saw something, and she's turning her head, craning her neck, looking back, trying hard to see.

IT'S NOT quite dark yet. Almost, but not quite. And because of that, she could make out the faces of the two people in the front seat of the car they passed.

Unless she was hallucinating.

Unless her brain is playing mean tricks on her.

Unless it's too ridiculous to be true.

"Vince, stop," she says.

"What?"

"Stop the car. Please. We need to turn around."

"How come?"

She shakes his arm. "Come on, please? Just do it. I think I saw . . . I don't know. I don't want to say yet. But let's turn around and see."

"See what?" he asks as he pulls into a driveway and then puts it in reverse. "Can you give me a hint?"

"No. Just go back the way we came."

And so that's what Vince does. When they turn the corner, the car they passed is now sitting in Carl's driveway. And Carl is running from the car to the spot where Trinity is standing, her face a perfect mixture of surprise and happiness.

Vince stops the BMW in front of the house and they both watch as Carl gathers his wife into his arms and covers her face with kisses.

"Wow," Vince whispers. "He's here." Emerson slowly opens her door. "Em? Where are you going? I think maybe we need to give them—"

But she doesn't let him finish. She walks toward the other car, her heart racing and her mind telling her it can't be. That it doesn't make sense and how could it *possibly* be true?

She remembers Trinity's words. *Let's stop trying to figure out everything and just be happy we're here.*

Is Emerson happy about this, though? If it's real, if it's true, will she be happy?

When she sees Frankie's face as she turns and looks at Emerson, out the side window, she feels a hundred different things in that moment, but mostly she *does* feel happy. She's missed her older sister, after all. Maybe she didn't even realize how much until this moment.

Frankie screams, "Emerson!" before she jumps out of the car and grabs her, pulling her into a hug. "Oh my God," Frankie says, her arms wrapped tightly around her sister. "I can't believe it. You're here. You're really here."

Emerson lets herself feel the love as tears pool in her eyes. She tries to find the words. The right words, to let her know how badly she feels.

"Frankie," she says as she pulls away and looks her sister in the eyes. She hasn't changed much. She's taller, maybe. Her hair's a little different, as she has bangs now, where she didn't before. But her eyes—her hazel eyes with rings of gold around the center—are still the same.

Emerson swallows hard. "I went to Dad's house, and I went into our room. I saw all the notes, and I want you to know, I didn't mean to hurt you. Please know that. I didn't think you cared that much, I guess, and I'm so sorry. About what I've put you through."

Now tears fill Frankie's eyes and she blinks quickly to try to keep them back. "If you didn't think I cared that much, then I'm the one who should be sorry. Truly. I get it. You didn't think you had any other choice but to leave. You felt like you had no one on your side." Now the tears fall. "But I was on your side, Em. I was always on your side. I just didn't do a very good job of letting you know that."

She pulls Emerson into her arms again as both of them cry. They stay that way for a minute, until Frankie pulls away and says, "I think there are some other people here who want their turn."

Fear grips Emerson hard, so she clings to her sister as they turn to face their parents, who are now standing in Carl's driveway along with everyone else.

Her dad runs over to Emerson and pulls her into his arms, kissing her cheek as he does. "I'm so glad you're okay, sweetheart," he whispers in her ear. "I'm sorry. About everything. The rest doesn't matter right now. You're here, you're all right, and that's the important thing."

She can't find any words, so she gives a little nod. When he pulls away, he steps back and Emerson stares at the ground, afraid to look her mother in the eye.

"Oh, Emerson," her mom says, rushing over to her. "I can't even tell you how happy I am to see you."

When she hugs her mother, she takes in the familiar scent of coffee and hair spray as a mixture of happiness and fear washes over her. Happy because despite everything that happened between them, this is her mother. Now and always.

And terrified because she doesn't want to get hurt again. Not like that. Never again.

Emerson doesn't let the hug last more than a few seconds. She pulls away and finally looks at her mother, and waits. Waits to see what she has to say.

Her mom presses her hand against Emerson's cheek. "I don't expect you to forgive me, but I want you to know that I am sorry. I didn't handle things well. I didn't know what to do, honey. I felt like I had to choose, and obviously, I didn't choose well. I want you to know he's out of the picture now. He moved out. It's just me and your sisters." Her face lights up. "Oh! You have to see Paige. You won't believe how big she's gotten."

Her mom quickly moves to the car and opens the door to the backseat. After a couple of clicks and some gentle maneuvering, Paige is out of her car seat and in her mother's arms.

"Paige, this is your sister Emerson. Can you say hi?"

"Hi," she says easily and effortlessly. Her big blue eyes and blond curls are so cute, Emerson can hardly contain herself.

"Hi, Paige," Emerson says. She puts her arms out. "Can I hold you?"

And when the adorable two-year-old climbs into Emerson's arms, and Emerson puts her cheek against Paige's sweet, soft skin, a feeling of pure contentment washes over her. The feeling stirs up a memory, like a flash, that comes from long ago—of curling up in a chair with a good book and wanting nothing else than to spend time in the story. She is here, in her own story, and even with all the strange twists and turns, she's so very glad about that.

Emerson closes her eyes and lets herself enjoy the feeling. And that's when she thinks of Vince, because he's a part of her happiness, too.

"Oh my gosh," she says, handing Paige back to her mother. "There's someone you guys have to meet."

But when she turns to the street, to wave Vince over, he's gone, along with the fancy BMW.

*She runs*

**DOWN THE** street.
Around the corner.

Searching.
        Wishing.
                Wondering.

*Why
did
you
go?*

Daylight disappears.
Darkness settles in.

Is this
what death
feels like?

"LET'S GO home," her mother says.

*Home.*

Just the mention of that one word, and the memory comes rushing back. When she and Vince were in the library.

*It's not about going home. It's about the feeling. The feeling of being home.*

Why is it so hard to see things when they are right in front of you? She didn't need to go anywhere.

She had it all along. When she was with Vince, she was home.

On the streets.

In the shelter.

In a BMW.

He was her home. Because home isn't where you are so much as it's who you are with.

Emerson shakes her head, hard. "No. I can't go. I can't leave. He might come back here. Or maybe he's close by. I have to try and find him." She looks in her mother's eyes, pleading. "Don't you understand? I have to."

She hears Frankie sniffle behind her, and the sudden knowledge that she's causing them pain all over again makes her stomach feel like she's swallowed a thousand needles.

And then, Carl is there. "I have an idea. Why don't you all come inside? Just for a little while? Maybe he'll come back.

Maybe he wanted to give you some time alone. If he doesn't come back soon, then you can go. How's that sound?"

"I think that sounds like a good plan," her mother says. "Emerson? What do you say?"

She can't get her brain to stop thinking, *Why?*

Why did he go? Why'd he leave without saying good-bye? Why did he think she'd want things to be this way?

Frankie comes and puts her arm around Emerson's waist. "We're going inside," she says firmly. "We'll wait here for a while. I'm not going home without you, all right? You don't get to decide everything anymore. It's not just about you."

Emerson lets herself be led into the house. She hears someone rattling around in the kitchen as they take a seat at the dining room table. The stereo plays a familiar song by the Beatles.

"This is really unbelievable," Carl says as he sits across from Emerson. "That you ended up here, of all places. May I ask you how that happened, exactly?"

Emerson nervously rubs her hands together. "We wanted a nice place to wait things out. We thought your house would be empty. Otherwise, you wouldn't have been . . . there. Where we found you."

Carl nods. "So you came here. And you found Trinity."

"Right. It surprised us. But she told us she talked to you on the phone after we left. But what I want to know is how you ended up with my family?"

So he tells her what happened. Tells her about Jerry. About getting knocked out. About being saved by her mom and sister.

Trinity appears as he's telling the story, carrying plates and forks. She passes them out as she listens. And then she returns to the kitchen and brings out a beautiful quiche on a gorgeous scalloped white cake stand.

When Carl finishes his story, Emerson's mother compliments Trinity on the quiche.

"I had all the time in the world today," she explains. "Decided I might as well put it to good use. You know, all of you ending up here at the same time, it's like the perfect storm. But in a good way."

"The perfect miracle," Frankie says.

"Before the perfect tragedy," Emerson says drily. "Unless the skeptics are right, I guess."

Her mother gives her a curious look. "What skeptics?"

"Vince and I learned earlier today that there are people out there who believe this is all a giant hoax. They think it's the government, wanting to push the reset button or something."

Her father shakes his head. "It takes all kinds, I guess."

"Well, shall we have a little supper?" Trinity asks. She hands Carl the serving pieces. "Can you cut it for me, please? I'm going to get everyone some juice."

"I feel like I should go look for Vince," Emerson says. "So I can kill him with my own bare hands."

Frankie laughs, startling Paige, who is sitting on her lap, playing with a stuffed monkey. "Glad to see you haven't lost your sense of humor."

"It's dark out, Em," her dad says. "I don't like the idea of you going out there."

"Have a bite to eat," her mom says. "If he hasn't come back, maybe we can all drive around and look for him. How's that?"

Trinity brings four glasses and returns to the kitchen.

"Have you known each other long?" her mother asks. "You and Vince, I mean."

"Feels like I've known him forever," is all Emerson says. She doesn't want to tell them how long or about how they met or what the streets were like. They don't really want to know. Maybe they think they do, but they don't.

"Well, I'm glad you had someone looking after you," her dad says.

Trinity returns with two more glasses and a large pitcher of orange juice. While Carl passes out slices of the quiche, Trinity pours the juice.

"I'm curious," Carl says after everyone's served. "After you left the bridge, what did you do? Did you find any people to help, like we talked about?"

Emerson smiles. "Yeah. We did. We helped a kid become a rock star. And we took a woman to a place very much like Paris. And we took two girls to the Enchanted Forest earlier today."

"Aw, I love that place," Frankie says. "Did you go down the slide?"

"A bunch of times," she replies as she watches Frankie offer a forkful of food to Paige. Emerson turns to Carl. "We had so much fun, I can't even tell you. Thank you for that."

"You're welcome," he says. "I had fun, too. Makes the end a little easier to take, doesn't it?"

No one says anything, and the words hang there like an invisible noose. Rhonda turns her head, biting her lip, as she tries to compose herself, but eventually, she pushes her chair back and gets up.

"I'm sorry, but I can't do this," she says. "I can't sit here and pretend like everything's fine, when it's not. What the hell are we doing? We hardly have any time left, and we're stuffing our mouths with quiche? What kind of alternate universe are you all living in? This isn't a celebration. It's not like it's someone's birthday, for Christ's sake. We shouldn't be happy the world is about to end."

Emerson glances at Paige, wondering if her mother's outburst has made her anxious, but she's oblivious, lost in her own little world with her monkey.

"Well, obviously, it isn't someone's birthday," Emerson says, trying to ease the tension. "Otherwise we'd have cake. Preferably chocolate with raspberry filling."

Her mom ignores Emerson and looks at Trinity. "Can you point me to the restroom?"

"Here, I'll show you," Trinity says, putting her arm around Rhonda as they walk toward the hallway. Everyone else sits there, awkwardly.

"Well, this is not how I pictured it," Frankie says. "At all."

"I think we need something stronger than orange juice," James says to Carl as he stands up.

"Sure," Carl says, pointing to a cabinet in the living room. "Follow me."

Emerson stands up and looks at Frankie and Paige. Frankie stares at Emerson for a moment before she mouths the words, *Be careful*.

Emerson nods before she turns and hurries to the door. And just like that, she's gone.

Outside.

Alone for the first time in a long, long time.

BUT NOT for long. She stands there for a minute, trying to decide what direction to go, when the car pulls up.

The relief she feels is instant and deep. Her mind whispers the words, *Thank you, thank you, thank you* over and over again.

He gets out.

She walks over and yells, "You better have a really good reason for leaving, or I swear I'm going to kick your ass and hand it to you on a silver platter."

He tries to hold it in. He tries to hold back his laughter, but he can't. He laughs and laughs as she stands there, glaring at him.

She shakes her head. "It's not funny, Vince."

"Yes," he says. "You are. I'm sorry, but you are."

And then, she can't help but smile, too. Because she loves hearing him laugh. She loves that he's here, telling her she's funny when she's completely and totally pissed off. She loves him, period. And that's all there is to it.

"Don't you ever do that again," she says as she saunters up close to him. Gives him a kiss. "I thought you were gone forever."

"Girl, you can't get rid of me that easily. Don't you know that by now?"

"We almost left. Did you think about that? That we might leave, and go home? Luckily, Carl and Trinity invited us inside."

"I knew you wouldn't leave," he says. "I knew it'd be okay."

"How'd you know?"

"I just did. I figured you could have a little bit of time with your family while I went and did something for all of you. All of us."

"So, where'd you go?"

He opens the back door of the car and pulls out a guitar. "The next hour can either be heaven or hell. I say let's have a campfire, sing 'Kumbaya' or 'Country Roads' or whatever the hell you want with your family, and try for a little of the good stuff."

She stares at the guitar for a moment before she says, "Because there's more to a book than an ending?"

Then she moves close to him again, and this time, takes his face in her hands, as she stands on her toes and kisses his soft lips one more time.

"That's right," he says. "Way more. And there's still a lot of time to enjoy this story we're in."

"I'm sorry to say, at this point, there's really not, Mr. Exaggeration."

"Doesn't matter, remember?" he whispers. "We have right now. And that's enough."

She kisses him again, longer this time. Then she says, "A campfire? With my crazy family? Are you sure?"

"I'm sure," he says, pointing to the trunk. "I even got us some firewood."

"Do I want to know how you got this stuff?" she asks, eyeing him suspiciously.

"I didn't steal it, if that's what you're wondering."

"Well," she says after she thinks about it for a second, "I guess sitting around a campfire, singing songs, beats sitting around the table, crying, which is about what was happening before I came out here."

"Exactly," he says. "And remember how I promised I'd tell you if there's something you could do for me?"

"Yes."

"Green Day's 'Time of Your Life' was my mom's favorite. Will you sing it with me?"

She nods. "Of course."

"Good. Let's go. You can help carry the firewood into their backyard."

She goes around to the trunk and sees the five pieces of kindling. "I don't know, Vince. Are you sure this is safe? That's a lot of wood. We might burn the neighborhood down."

"Hey, it's all the guy had," he says. "Better than nothing, right?"

"Which guy?"

"The guy who gave me the guitar and the firewood, who do you think?"

Emerson smiles as she starts to pick up the wood, then stops. "But what if Carl and Trinity want to be alone? We're kind of invading their space, you know? Maybe we should ask them what they want to do."

"Okay," he says, setting the guitar in the trunk. "We can do that. If they don't want us hanging around, there's a park around the corner. The rest of us can go there."

Emerson imagines them sitting around the fire, watching it sizzle and pop as they listen to Vince play.

Maybe Paige will dance.

Maybe Frankie will sing like a star.

Maybe her mom will stop crying.

She can only hope.

"What should we sing first, to get warmed up?" Vince asks as he comes around and takes Emerson's hand.

"Well, if Trinity and Carl join us, maybe we should let Carl choose. Sounds like the guy's been to hell and back."

"At least he's here," Vince says.

Emerson looks up at the sky. The night is clear. The stars are bright. Incredibly vivid. "We could say the same about us, you know? Pretty amazing."

He runs his hand down her arm, making it tingle. "Incredibly amazing."

And then, they hear Frankie's voice, yelling in the night air. "Emerson!" The two of them turn and see Frankie in the driveway, waving her hand, motioning them to come inside. "Hurry! You have to get in here. You're not going to believe what they're saying on the radio."

Emerson glances at Vince. His half grin is as cute as ever. He squeezes her hand and they both start running.

"You still like surprises?" he asks as they go.

"You're asking me that now?" Emerson says.

"Well, I still hate them," he says. "And right now, I'm dying to know how this story ends."

"It's hard to say," Emerson tells him. "But you gotta admit, whatever happens, the characters rocked it, didn't they?"

When the two of them reach the front door, they stop. They can hear chatter and laughter inside the house.

Like a birthday party.

A celebration.

Vince laughs. "Girl, those characters *totally* rocked it."

**WHILE A** whole lot has changed,
some things have remained the same.

The state fair is still
a fried-food mecca.

And a fresh strawberry milk shake
is summertime bliss in a cup.

Emerson and Vince race
tiny horses with squirt guns.

Vince wins a pink unicorn
and gives it to Emerson.

"Unicorns are magical," he says.
Just like time, with its ability to change things.

Emerson and Frankie now share a little apartment and
go to Portland Community College together.

Vince lives with Carl and Trinity.
He works at the café with Phillipe,

baking macarons and muffins,
and scones served with jam.

"Ready for the carousel?" Emerson asks.
Vince kisses her. "Ready. And after that, the Tilt-A-Whirl!"

Carousels still go around.
Second chances are real.

Wishes really do come true.
Stories end.

And new ones
begin . . .